Cornelia M. Speedy

My Wanderings in the Soudan

Volume 2

Cornelia M. Speedy

My Wanderings in the Soudan
Volume 2

ISBN/EAN: 9783337189563

Printed in Europe, USA, Canada, Australia, Japan

Cover: Foto ©Andreas Hilbeck / pixelio.de

More available books at **www.hansebooks.com**

MY WANDERINGS IN
THE SOUDAN

BY MRS. SPEEDY

HAMRAN ARABS

IN TWO VOLUMES—VOL. II.

LONDON

RICHARD BENTLEY & SON, NEW BURLINGTON ST.

Publishers in Ordinary to Her Majesty the Queen

1884

CONTENTS.

LETTER XXXI.

LETTER XXXII.

ILLUSTRATIONS.

LETTER XVII.

KASSALA, 15*th March.*

AFTER the feast which I described in my last
was over, we all adjourned into the courtyard
again, where quite a transformation scene had
taken place. It was a large piece of ground,
and there were several trees in it. On these,
in and about among the branches, coloured
lamps both of paper and glass of all shapes
and sizes were hung, and as it was getting
dark, they had just been lighted. The bright
hues of these lamps shone out splendidly, and
the effect was really very pretty.

Larger and better pieces of matting than
those which had been there before were placed
in the centre of the yard, and round these the
benches were again ranged. We were all

soon seated, and then from one end of the
ground a procession of girls in pure white
muslin wound their way to the front, and commenced dancing on the matting which had
been laid down. There were eight or ten of
them, and they began together forming slow
movements, which reminded me in a way of
our own quadrille ; but very soon all but four
sat down on each side and waited, while this
quartette pirouetted about ; then two only
danced together, going through all sorts of
queer and fantastic motions, and becoming
much more animated than when there had
been greater numbers : they flung their arms
over their heads, placed them akimbo on their
hips, erected themselves to the very extremity
of their toes, bent their bodies backwards and
forwards to an alarming extent, and passed and
repassed each other repeatedly.

Sometimes they sang a low sort of mono-
tonous chant, which, at unexpected intervals,
broke into an excited cry ; but for the most
part they danced in silence. At last one only
was left, and when that one became the sole
object of attention she did her utmost to sur-
pass every previous exhibition of agility. Yet
in spite of the springs and bounds that were

achieved, and the marvellous positions into which her supple body was twisted, there was scarcely any movement which was not graceful, and there was very little dissimilarity in my opinion between these black-eyed lithe-limbed nymphs and the best trained ballet-girls to be seen on any European stage.

This dancing continued for a long time, and I got quite tired of it, as there was very little variation in the different styles, and it came at last to be simply a matter of competition between the performers. Each one of those that had already sat down had her turn alone, and when they had all exhausted their powers, or the spectators had wearied of seeing them, others (non-professionals, so to speak), guests from among the crowd, stood up and did their best in the same way to entertain the company. Even Madame (the Italian) danced! and though her performance was not nearly equal to even the most mediocre of her forerunners, she received the only applause that was given; approving glances and words of commendation being also directed to me all the time; this applause was expressed by satisfied murmurs, but no clapping took place, and I feel sure that our kind hostesses designed the approbation as a compliment and sign of goodwill to us both as foreigners; it may have been that as we spoke the same language to each other, our dark neighbours imagined we belonged to the same country.

Finally, to my great satisfaction, the dancing came to an end, and then occurred the closing ceremony of the evening, which was wholly characteristic of the country, and totally unlike anything I had ever seen. It had relation only to the rite which was to take place next day, and was "the procession of *henna*." While the dancing was going on innumerable little wax tapers of a very rude construction had been stuck into the ground all round the courtyard. In some places these were two or three rows deep, and they not only went round the yard, but in many other directions; round the trees, the house, even round the cook-houses, and others were mapped out to form fantastic shapes and grotesque patterns in different parts of the ground.

To begin with, the eldest boy, whom I before alluded to, had singly and by himself, probably as deputy for both his brothers, to light all these tapers, and it was well for the child that what might have seemed to an onlooker to be a work of fatigue and labour, was regarded by him as one of fun and excitement. The only heart-breaking part of the business was that there was a slight breeze which blew out some of the tiny lamps repeatedly, so that it was really difficult to achieve what was considered a sufficient illumination before the procession began. This was, however, at last accomplished, and then came another curious event. A large dish filled with a deep red-coloured paste, made from the leaves of a plant called "*henna*," was brought out by one of the women, whose especial charge it seemed to be, and the forehead, cheeks, chin, and hands of all three children, as well as those of any of the guests who wished it, were thickly smeared with this horrid-looking stuff.

Lighted torches were then put into the hands of the two elder boys, while their mother, with the baby in her arms, carried one in its stead ; many other torches and large lighted tapers and lanterns were borne by an indiscriminate multitude of the guests, and all set off together to make repeated tours round the courtyard. This parade was not accomplished in silence; they chanted in most excited accents —accompanying their song with wild gestures and much flourishing about of the torches as they marched—a long and dismal hymn in praise of henna. They hold this plant in almost superstitious awe, and regard it as the infallible cure for many ills. It was a wild and curious spectacle, and they looked a weird strange party as they passed along.

One part of it, however, distressed me much. After the procession had come to an end, and the tapers and torches were nearly all extinguished, the children's hands were tied up in bags, from which, however irritating the paste with which their faces were besmeared might become, as it was sure to do, they were forbidden under any consideration to extricate them until after the ceremony, which was not to take place till the next morning, was over. When that was accomplished the henna would be washed off. It is this same henna which is used all over the East for dyeing the nails ; it gives them a reddish orange colour, which Easterns consider extremely beautiful.

With the conclusion of this procession the evening's entertainment was at an end; the guests were leaving, and I felt sure that the poor tired lady of the house must be thoroughly worn out and greatly in need of rest. I had

misgivings, however, about the sort of night
she would be likely to pass with that sickly-
looking, fretful baby beside her, especially in
the trying condition in which I had last seen
it. We said good-bye, and I endeavoured to
express not only the real thanks I felt for all
the kindness I had received, but also the true
interest I had taken in all that I had witnessed.
As we went into the outer courtyard Charlie
was just emerging from the other side, so both
entertainments had closed at the same time ; he
said, however, that theirs had only consisted in
dining, talking, and smoking ; and though he
owned to having joined the feast all through
in true Arab style, and to having enjoyed it
thoroughly, nevertheless I considered that I had
had by far the best part of the evening—the
dance, the illuminations, and the henna procession having fallen to my share.

One fact in Arab life came to my notice that
day which I must not forget to tell you of. It
struck me as extremely melancholy. While I
was on the dais before the dinner, chatting with
some of the merry throng, and while others
were moving gaily about hither and thither
below, I noticed one young woman sitting quite
still and in a mournful attitude, looking de-

pressed and forlorn ; she was not on the dais but on the ground, and had a dejected expression that could scarcely escape notice.

I did not ask any questions, but Madame, who knew every one, saw that I observed her, and told me that she was the discarded wife of an Arab of good position. The poor thing had done nothing to raise her lord's ire ; she was not divorced nor an outcast in any way ; he had simply become tired of her and sent her back to her old home. They assured me that this often occurred, and there seemed to be no redress for it ; but no one, they said, would ever dream of marrying one of these rejected wives again—a slur was cast on them, and they were considered beneath any man's notice. I was told that though this circumstance was not unusual, a deep melancholy always settled on the sad victim of the heartless freak, and I could not but feel deep indignation with a condition of lawlessness which permits so cruel a custom.

We reached home about eleven o'clock, and though very tired I felt well satisfied with my first day's " outing " in Kassala, but I did little else than rest all the next day ; the heat was very oppressive, and I felt very feverish. In the morning a rap came to the door, and on

opening it I saw Madame, with two Arab
women, standing outside; she inquired cautiously if Charlie were within, and on my saying
he was, she made a sign to the two ladies, who
drew the already thickly concealing chuddah
still more closely over their hidden faces, and
moved off to one side in the passage, turning
their backs to the doorway.

She then explained to me that they were of
very high rank, and of a very strict sect in
religion, and must on no account be seen by a
strange man—especially one who was of another
nation and an infidel.   They were, however,
very anxious to see *me*, and had come to do me
that honour, and if Charlie would not object to
go below, or into some other room for a few
minutes, they would make their visit very short.
I represented the state of the case, and he at
once consented to absent himself, his only
regret being that he should not be able to converse with these ladies, as there were many
things he wished specially to know pertaining
to their religion, and which he was not likely to
have any opportunity so good as the present for
ascertaining.   I accordingly, in turn, represented
this side of the question to Madame, and after
much hesitation and whispered confabulations

in the passage a compromise was effected ; it being arranged that, completely veiled, the ladies should enter the room, not venturing to turn their heads in the direction of the masculine heathen, and that he should, before they entered, religiously turn his back to the direction by which they would come in ! This was all strictly carried out, and thus, back to back, and a considerable distance apart from each other, an edifying conversation went on for about half an hour—questions being put in bland, inquiring tones, and dulcet replies given, which appeared quite satisfactory to both parties. The effect was so ludicrous that, in spite of my utmost desire to bring my best manners to the front, I felt that I should be unable to restrain my laughter, so, after the first few moments, I retired discreetly to the passage, and beheld the never-to-be-forgotten scene from afar off.

You would be astonished if you could see a couple of shops or stores here, in the principal street, which are kept by Italian merchants. In the midst of this desert, where everything has to be brought either into or out of the country on camels, making transport both diffi- cult and expensive, these enterprising foreigners have imported all sorts of luxuries. Bass's beer,

Allsopp's ale, and spirituous liquors (you will grieve to hear); Huntley and Palmer's biscuits, Moir's preserves; even tinned provisions, such as Oxford sausages and haricot beans and asparagus, are some of the articles we came across this morning. I have actually found a bridle, too, as I hoped to, for " Prince." I can't say much for it! but it is better considerably than the one I had, and I was glad to get it.

Then, too, there are all kinds of cotton stuffs. I am sure they are "Manchester cottons!" the quality is generally extremely indifferent; the manufacturers evidently clear out all their rubbish when these goods are exported, and there are also some curious specimens of execrable cutlery—knives of "sorts," and a few carpenter's tools, but all of such bad steel—if indeed it is steel at all, and not merely iron—that they could not be relied upon for any hard or difficult work.

There are among the Egyptian, and even Arab officers belonging to the troops throughout the Soudan, several who have been to Europe, especially to France and Germany, and one or two even to London; and these men have a keen appreciation of all the comforts of civilisation, and encourage the importation of

such articles as these. They also, there is little
doubt, in spite of the prohibitions of their
religion, know quite well the meaning of malt
liquors and spirits, though these little delinquencies are kept strictly in the background.
One of these travelled officers is as handsome
a man as I have ever beheld. He is tall, very
well made, with regular features and magnificent
eyes; and possesses absolute grace of manner
and the most perfectly courteous bearing that
it would be possible for a man to have. He
paid me an early call one morning soon after
we arrived, and I was quite fascinated with
him! and deeply regretted that I was unable to
converse with him as fluently as I should like
to have done. He is called " Bim Bashi,"—
that is not his *name* (I have not a notion what
that is), it is only his title, and, I think, indicates
that he has command over a thousand soldiers.

I hear, alas! that he is a *great rascal!* and
has twice been cashiered for embezzlement of
the public money; but I cannot think harshly
of him all the same, and feel inclined to forgive him almost any iniquity on account of
his superb appearance and general fascination!
He looks *regal*, mounted on a splendid black
charger,—a creature that almost rivals his

master for beauty; indeed, he has made such an impression on me that I might be said to have Bim Bashi "*on the brain*"!

Almost immediately after he had left we had a call from a very different sort of visitor—a semi-countryman of our own—a forlorn Scotchman, who has been settled here for a number of years, and who, having seen every kind of vicissitude, and having lost one arm, poor man, has tried to retrieve his broken fortunes by establishing a saw-mill in the town, and is doing a precarious business in that line.

It was nice to hear one's own language again, and we were glad to be able to give such slight consolation as a sympathetic hearing and the ordering of a few boxes could afford; but the striking contrast between our two visitors told, as far as externals are concerned, sadly in favour of the Mohammedan, and if I were inclined to moralise, I should say some trite thing like, How grievous it is that worth and beauty do not always go hand in hand!

Charlie presented the Scotchman with a saw, and we consulted him about timber for building houses for us to live in during the rains; but as yet we are quite undecided as to what locality we shall settle in for that season.

It has been a woeful disappointment to me
to find that there is no such thing as laundry
work understood here.   They have not the
faintest idea of either starching or ironing, and
the washing even is done in the roughest way.
The very first day of our arrival I made inquiries as to this important item, and Madame
told me she would send me the best laundress
in the town ; and, accordingly, the next morning
she arrived.   Washerwomen, as a rule, are not
famed for beauty, but this one surpassed all for
ugliness that I have ever beheld.   Wizened,
though not particularly old, with a skin to
which the hide of a hippopotamus might almost
be considered dainty ! with every possible shade
of brown, red, black, and yellow in her face, she
was a perfect "study," though I can scarcely
imagine that even an artist would wish to
obtain such a subject, unique as it was.   She
entered, this poor old piece of care-worn,
poverty-battered humanity, and if any senti-
ment could be discerned amid the folds of her
wrinkled visage, I thought I became aware of
a kindly grin confronting me.   I responded
with a smile, into which I endeavoured to
throw a reassuring welcome (in one sense she
was very welcome), and I am always anxious

to make all these good folk feel at home with us; and we set to work to count out the things. To have identified them in any way but by number would have been impossible, for I imagine she had never seen the like of any of them at all before, and as to their actual design, save that they were clothing, she may be puzzling over it to this hour without having arrived at a right conclusion. So we just counted them,—so many pieces; she then rammed them all into a huge sack, slung it over her shoulder, gave me another friendly grin, and waddled off. I looked after her, marvelling in what condition they would return!

At the end of the third day she reappeared with the identical sack, slung in the same manner over her shoulder, in which she had taken it away. I began to fear that nothing had been done; but this was a cruel injustice; she told me she had "laboured at them all the time," and had made them "beautiful."

The *beauty* was then displayed; *en masse*, regardless of shape or quality, she hauled them out,—washed certainly, and redolent of soap still, but oh! what colours!—her own variegated face was reflected in softened hues in every one; as to smoothness, "*rough dried*" would have been a mild term by which to express their harshness. I wondered how we were ever to put them on; and I at once saw what kind of clean clothes we were to expect during the rest of our stay in the Soudan.

I thanked her, paid her, and told her to come back again in a couple of days. Then I set to work, and for the next hour Sher Ullah and myself were both fully employed. I separated all Charlie's things from mine, and gave them to him. As we have only a small camp table, I chose one of the biggest boxes, had it thoroughly dusted, and then made him spread out article by article on the top, and iron them, so to speak, with his hands—first of all rubbing out the harshness (which was partly due to the wretched limy soap they had been washed with) as well as he could, and folding them and pressing them down in a sort of make-believe mangling fashion, while I did the same with my own.

This process improved matters a little, and by the time they were finished they presented, I assure you, a very different appearance from that which they had had when the poor old ogress had brought them in.

LETTER XVIII.

Last letter from Kassala—Waterless desert in prospect—Arab ladies at home—Visit to the Pasha's wife—A curious superstition—Reserve in the Pasha's presence—Birthday of Mohammed—Grand parade—Bim Bashi again—Flirtation—Awake all night—Madame's farewell visit.

KASSALA, 17*th March.*

THIS will be my last from Kassala, I feel nearly sure, for unless anything very unexpected occurs we shall start to-morrow, and go forth through the parching desert again, *en route* for Jira, or Djira, as it is sometimes spelt, an Arab settlement on the river Settit. The Settit is called also the Atbara, or Black Nile. The Arabic name is *Bahr el Aswad,* "the black river"—*Bahr* being "river," *el* "the," and *Aswad* "black."

We shall have new experiences on the road, and some that I don't much relish the idea of, for during a part of the route there is a three days' march with no water whatever to be found—no wells; in fact, we shall traverse a waterless desert, and shall have to take the supply for our whole party in skins on camels, and to economise it as much as possible.

The heat in the town has been far worse of late than it was at first, and the dust is terrific. It blows in through the ill-fitting venetians, even if we have them closed, and smothers everything; but, indeed, we very rarely close them entirely, for then not only is it too dark to see to do anything, but also the air, from want of circulation, becomes so stifling that it is almost impossible to breathe, and one feels choking. Nevertheless, while we have been in a house, such as it is, we have had shelter from the blazing heat, and discomforts have been in the minimum, so I must not grumble. I must, however, tell you of a curious disturbance I have experienced at night, which, from the circumstance I mentioned with regard to the graves, you will scarcely be surprised at. It is the noise of the hyenas as they rove in numbers through the streets. The people appear to be quite regardless of them,—indeed, they are looked upon as scavengers,—and they accompany their wanderings with the most horrible howlings that make me shudder as I hear them!

I have been to all the houses of the principal

Arab ladies with Madame to make "afternoon calls!" and also to visit the wife of the Pasha; so, besides the great entertainment at the Commandant's house, I have really seen all the home-life of Kassala, and it has been excessively interesting.

I have found the Arab ladies, sometimes most refined both in appearance and manners, clean, dressed generally in snowy, soft, white muslin, and always glad to see us. They often do embroidery, especially working lovely borders, in silk and gold thread, for their flowing garments; and they showed us their work, when we asked to see it, without the least bombast or vanity. The inmates of one house especially, I shall never forget — an old lady, her daughter, and her son's wife (the latter is a widow), and they are all in their own way perfect ladies. The *dowager* is quite a picture, and the other two women are extremely handsome, and I wished much that I could have photographed them all. We were entertained with coffee, which a servant brought from a kitchen not in sight, without an order, almost immediately on our arrival; and everything was done in a quiet refined manner, that indicated a tone very much above the general run. Coffee always appeared at every house, but very often the hostess prepared it herself in our presence ; and I have come to see how even in Kassala there are grades of rank and different social positions.

The Pasha's wife is a pretty, fair Circassian ; far fairer than most Europeans! and it was strange and unexpected to see this delicate woman, with a pink-and-white complexion, in a land of swarthy skins. I was informed that to be taken to see her was a great honour, as she is considered of such extreme importance, and in consequence so unapproachable, that but few of the Arab ladies are ever allowed to visit her!—the result of this high valuation being that she lives in seclusion, for which no dignity, I should imagine, could possibly compensate. She is not allowed to go out either, not having been beyond the gates of her garden for more than seven years, as it is not considered the right thing that she should be seen out of her home ; her position appeared to me to be little better than that of solitary confinement ; and being a gentle timid woman, her life of restraint has probably taken away what little spirit she may have ever possessed. Happily for her, after several years of married life, she had a baby boy, and this child, which is about eighteen months old, was brought in by an Arab nurse. I cannot say that it is a pretty child; but the mother, poor thing, beamed radiantly upon it, and it seemed to be her one joy in life. Madame did most of the conversation, translating for me into Arabic whatever I wished to say, which I told her, to begin with, in French. Coffee was *twice* brought, also several " drinks " of various kinds, including very delicious sherbet, and a sort of rose water, quite different from anything else I had ever tasted. As we made a long (shall I say wearisomely long ?) visit, this being considered the proper etiquette, there was plenty of time for these successive hospitalities, and they even formed a pleasing diversion in the quiet monotony. A curious superstition came to my knowledge during this visit, which is strangely opposed to our English ideas. I was beginning to take notice of, and even, I fear, to perjure my own conscience slightly, in favour of the young heir of the establishment, thereby hoping to bring pleasure to the mother's heart, when I was abruptly stopped by Madame, who begged me on no account to do anything of the sort, as it was considered extremely unlucky to take any

special notice of, or to praise any child, particularly one in high rank ; the idea being, as far
as I could gather, that to do so was "tempting
Providence" to remove it ! and that the charms
of ever so great a treasure must pass unobserved,
or ill fortune would assuredly descend upon the
happy but unfortunate possessor.

On taking our leave the lady accompanied
us through the garden, which was about two
acres in extent and in very tolerable order,
full of water-melons, citron and orange trees,
and well stocked with luscious vegetables,
bowery creepers, and many kinds of palms
which, with seats under them, made pleasant
cool places for early morning or evening resort ;
and I was glad to find that the "*State Prisoner*"
had such good grounds, though even they must
have palled terribly upon her after such a lapse
of years.   As she was walking with us towards
the gates she suddenly descried the " Pasha "
arriving from the quarter for which we were
making, and at once, with a slight murmur,
dropped behind us, and so remained until and
after he met us, moving about in the background, while we were talking to him, in a
nervous timid manner, looking like a frightened
fawn, and not venturing a word ; and when we

had said good-bye to him and turned to shake hands again with her, she seemed almost afraid to return our adieu, or to acknowledge that she was there.

Madame told me that it was scarcely etiquette for her to be seen in our presence—although we were women—by her husband; and that it was a proof of his being really very kind and indulgent to her that she had ventured to remain near us at all! The lonely life of that poor Circassian lady, and the apprehension that there must be many in a position similar to hers, will haunt me for many a long day.

Yesterday, the 16th, was the birthday of Mohammed the prophet — the founder and author of Mohammedanism—and all the city was astir with rejoicings and celebrations, so we had an opportunity of witnessing a great public demonstration. About four o'clock in the afternoon Madame called for me and took me with her to the telegraph office, from one of the windows of which we had a splendid view of all the greatest doings on the occasion. This office forms part of a block of public buildings, overlooking a large square, and adjoins the Diwan, with which I first made acquaintance on the day of my entrance into Kassala.

The celebrations began at eleven in the morning, the first ceremony being a religious service in the Mosque at that hour; this had been preceded by "roll-call," and an ordinary parade of the troops; an interval of rest had occurred between one o'clock and three, but at that time a very much more important parade, accompanied by all manner of manœuvres and strict inspection by the Pasha, took place. This was still going on when we took up our posts on the telegraph window-sill, which was fortunately broad enough to accommodate us without much inconvenience, though the sort of side-way we were obliged to screw ourselves into, and the straight board or front of the sill, I at last found to be very tiring.

Manœuvre followed manœuvre, all more or less alike, none very brilliantly performed, and each I own to having found more or less wearisome; but still I was expected to remain and to take fresh delight in each succeeding one! Charlie was with the Pasha below (in the highest post of honour!), moving about with the officers, and in the midst of the general animation,—passing commendations, and being

asked even for criticisms ; but I fear, nevertheless, that he found it scarcely more interesting
than I did, and was equally longing for the
parade to be over. The band of the Kassala
garrison tootled out its best the whole time, in
the squeakiest and shrillest of fifes and other
instruments, the monotony of the ever-recurring
tune being the chief feature of the music, and
the one which I shall certainly never forget!
and I was earnestly longing that the time for
fireworks, which were to crown the proceedings,
would arrive, when a most pleasing diversion
occurred in the unexpected appearance below
the window of the beautiful " Bim Bashi."

He was as magnificent as ever ; but, alas ! I
very soon discovered that I could in no way
attribute the cause of his arrival to *my* presence,
but, on the contrary, to that of Madame ; and
it quickly became evident that she had long
been an object of attraction to this Adonis, and
that an old-standing intimacy existed between
them. After a mere interchange of civilities
on my part, which was almost as far as my
imperfect Arabic would take me, I subsided
into an amused spectator of the very animated
flirtation that then took place, which, from her
fluent knowledge of the language, was an easy

matter; and had to content myself with the recreation afforded me by *that*, and the very welcome coffee that now appeared—and for which, I was perfectly aware, we were indebted to this friendship !

It subsequently transpired that Madame carried this cordiality to the point of acting as Bim Bashi's laundress! and that his exquisite linen, which I had before admired with amazement, was *her* handiwork, she undertaking to "get up" his shirts in true continental style.

In course of time, however, he had again to rejoin his companies, the troops were to my joy dismissed, and by and by it grew dusk enough for the illuminations to commence. These were really very fine, and amazing for Kassala (an Arab town in the midst of a far-away desert)! Lanterns of every description, naturally far more numerous and brilliant in colour than those that had been displayed at the Commandant's house, were hung in every direction. Lamps of many kinds were lighted, and the whole ground was bordered with little wicks in oil, of the same kind as those which were round the other courtyard.

A great display of fireworks, which were passable and abundant, but not very brilliant, then took place, and two balloons were sent up; the whole fête closing with another prolonged and extra-shrill rattle and battle of fifes and drums, which ended this celebration of the prophet's birth.

Up to the hour I had gone out to see this great fête I had been busy packing all day, preparatory to a start which we hope to make to-morrow, so you may imagine that I was pretty tired by the time we got home, and that I was more than ready for the supper that was awaiting us; for we had had nothing (save the coffee provided by Bim Bashi) since our lunch breakfast at one o'clock, and it was now close upon midnight.

Very much done up I lay down, hoping for a good night's rest, but, alas, for the effect of that fascinating officer's kind attention! Probably with a view to the well-seasoned taste of Madame, the coffee that was sent us was even stronger than that I had usually been regaled with, and the effect was that I never closed my eyes all night. Feverish and restless I tossed about, longing for the sleep which would not come, and listening to the hyenas! About four o'clock I sank into a doze, but awoke at six, and finding further sleep impossible, got up

and went out for what I imagine will be my
last early morning walk in Kassala.

18*th*. We shall be off this evening, I believe. Madame came this morning to pay us
her last visit and to say good-bye ; for she
knew I should be probably too busy to come
out. She has been a good friend, and, as I
said before, it has been truly lucky for me that
I found her here, otherwise I should have
known and seen nothing of the Arab life that
has now been revealed to me. I shall always
feel truly indebted to her, and through her
kindness shall ever have a most interesting and
pleasant recollection of my visit to Kassala.

LETTER XIX.

HAMZA'S ZAREEBA; ON THE SETTIT,
23d March.

I DON'T know how I shall manage to get
through all I have to tell you of what has
occurred since my last letter. The days have
been crowded with incidents, but the marching has been so very hard that it was utterly
impossible to write; we have scarcely halted
till now since leaving Kassala, and each night
I have been so "dead done up" that at last I
have been scarcely able to sleep at all, so you
can realise how very fatiguing the travelling
has been.

We were obliged to press on in hot haste on
account of the want of water in the country that
I alluded to in my last; and, owing to this same

want, we were solely dependent for our supply on what we took with us. We left Kassala about seven o'clock on the evening of the 18th, and went on till half-past eleven. About a mile from the town we passed under a mountain nearly four thousand feet high— one huge bare mass of granite. There are many deep caves and long recesses on the sides of this mountain (and also at the foot), formed by natural hollows in the stone, and these caverns are the haunts of robbers who congregate there to plunder the caravans that go past.

The Egyptian Government either cannot or will not put them down, and they are the terror of all travellers. Our men did not for a moment conceal their fear that we might be attacked, and were most urgent that we should keep all close together, and that rifles should be repeatedly fired off.

I was riding "Prince" again, and the great difficulty was to keep him close to the others, for his long rest has made him so fresh that he was for galloping ahead, and I had much ado to restrain his ardour! Had I let him go he might have cantered himself and me off into the very teeth of the enemy before the others could possibly come up to our rescue! However, I got him well up into the centre of the cavalcade, where, in spite of his pulling, he found passing pretty difficult.

It was a splendid moonlight night, and the stars, too, were as clear as possible, so *that* was greatly in our favour, and I am happy to say that no one attacked us, though alarms concerning those that were supposed to be lying in wait were numerous; and certainly the dark shadows in every direction under the mountain were not reassuring. There were many trees, too, which, with their immense trunks and deep shade, added to the general nervousness, and I cannot but own that I felt more comfortable when we had passed that frowning hill and had got into the open, beyond it. The country then was very flat, and the soil extremely fine, like fuller's earth; the plain was covered with mimosa bushes, from which every leaf had long ago disappeared, and there was not anywhere a particle of shade. Near midnight we encamped close beside a small Arab village, all the houses of which were "birsch,"—that is, as I think I have before mentioned, made of matting. We had a small tent put up, and after a hasty supper of cold curry, cooked previously and carried in the lunch-basket to be ready when we halted, I

went to bed.   It seemed so curious next morning after the different sort of life we have had
for nearly a fortnight, which in reality had
appeared much longer, to be off upon the road
again at 6 A.M. ; but so we were, and at noon
we reached another birsch village, and dismounted to have a rest under a birsch tent
till the severe heat was passed.   We were so
warmly received that it was quite gratifying,
and I am ungrateful enough to add not a little
overpowering.

All the men of the village came crowding
into the small hut which had been placed at
our disposal, and the atmosphere, which was
doing its best to stifle us without this assistance,
did not improve in consequence.   Charlie exhibited the wonders of a pistol, a kukri, a
chopper, his watch, and various other articles
of the kind, which to these good folk were
new, and the general wonder and admiration
were boundless.

I, too, was an object of much curiosity ; but
I had managed to ensconce myself on the angréb
I brought from Kassala, well in the background,
so my swarthy friends were obliged to inspect
me from afar off, and to be satisfied with the
distant view they got.   I smiled blandly at

them from my vantage-ground, but was too tired to enter into the general conversation.

After about an hour of this sort the head-man — the chief of the village, who was a very "superior person" indeed, really quite a nice fellow—disappeared for a few moments, and reappeared bringing us two splendid joints of mutton as a gift, and also water sweetened with honey in a beautiful gourd. Shortly after this the crowd dispersed, and the wife of the chief came to the door of the tent and asked for some brandy, alleging that one of her children was ill and needed it as medicine. We accordingly poured out a small quantity suitable for a child in such distress, but she looked this gift-horse in the mouth with such evident signs of dissatisfaction that Charlie divined that the plea of illness was a mere ruse, and that our liberal host had probably desired the tonic on his own account, but, reluctant to ask for it himself, had sent his wife to obtain the forbidden luxury; so we gave her enough to satisfy her lord, and, I fear, more than was good for him; and she took it off, rejoicing, to the depths of the village.

We remained resting in this little house of matting till about four o'clock, when we began to prepare for a fresh start. I forgot to tell you that we were not disappointed in being able to obtain at Kassala the good riding camels we had hoped for. We have two beauties; and I have been amazed to find that the pace of a well-bred, well-trained camel, is not in the least fatiguing, and that they are, in fact, delightful creatures to ride. Mine is the bigger of the two by far; he is also the gentler, and the better in every way (so you may be sure that he was apportioned to me from the first)! His name is " Wad Zaid," and already I love him dearly.[1] He is such an enormous great fellow that, before I mounted, I really could not help feeling a little timorous at the thought of being up so high,— far away from any possibility of aid should he take it into his head to execute any curious manœuvre pertaining to camel exercise that might baffle me; but I had not been on him two minutes before I found that he was perfectly reliable, and had evidently taken me in charge as an especial trust! He is so very tall and big that when we are mounted I am far above Charlie! and look down upon him from my giddy height in quite an amusing manner.

[1] Wad Zaid means "Son of Zaid," and is the name of a chief of the Dābāinā tribe, who formerly owned this dromedary.

I don't know whether you are aware that these good riding camels are *par excellence* "dromedaries." It is, I believe, a usual impression that a dromedary is a two-humped camel, but this is really not the case. A dromedary simply means a camel capable of moving very swiftly; and if you will look in my favourite dictionary (Stormonth's) you will find that it is there quite correctly described (*i.e.* "from Greek *dromas*, running, swift, the one-hump camel of Arabia, more swift of foot than the camel"); by which, of course, is meant the ordinary baggage camel, which might in distinction be said to be famed for its *slowness!* and, I should add, the roughness of its pace.

While I am speaking about the camels I must tell you how we mount and dismount them, and what their saddles and bridles are; for though these points have now all become so familiar to myself that it seems to me almost presumptuous to suppose you do not know about them just as well as I do, it suddenly strikes me that you may not, and that you may perhaps like to have an account of them. To begin with the mounting and dismounting. The camel always kneels while that goes on : but every camel always appears to hate kneeling on compulsion. Even the well-trained dromedaries seem to dislike doing it, and are not only sometimes difficult to get down and keep down, but they even occasionally offer a faint vocal remonstrance, though this is nothing to the appalling tumult which the baggage camels create while they are being laden. They are always so anxious to get up quickly that it not unfrequently happens that they will try to rise before one is well settled into the saddle, giving a violent jerk, first backwards and then forwards, and nearly pitching one off altogether, as these movements come quite un-expectedly, and before one is prepared for them. The servant who is holding the reins while one mounts usually places his foot lightly on the doubled-up leg of the kneeling camel as a sign to him that he is not to move; but should this be omitted, and the creature more than usually impatient, the startling result I have just men-tioned is almost sure to occur.

I am mounted exactly as I should be if I were mounting a horse, and there is what might be called a pommel,—two, indeed, but these are very different from what we understand at home as pommels. The saddle is a wooden construc-tion, which it is rather difficult to describe. It goes over the hump on the camel's back, and to fit this four separate, or two forked, pieces of wood, which form the stand on which the seat is supported, slope at acute angles towards each other till they meet, when, if they are separate, they are bound together with strips of leather. Two other pieces of wood are bound on to them in upright positions, one before and the other behind, and these form what I have ventured to call pommels ; between these uprights a curved or hollowed board is laid, which is the seat. Into this seat any number of cushions and pillows may be placed, and over all is thrown the delicious farrwah, which I think I have told you of before ; and one sits facing the camel's head, *on the top of the hump*, with one's feet crossed over the front pommel. The *farrwahs* are sometimes made from the skins of goats, which have particularly long silky hair, and this, when carefully prepared, becomes exquisitely fine and soft, and when it has been well bleached is beautifully white. Now for the bridles. For common baggage camels they are merely pieces of rope, but those for riding camels are made of plaited leather of different colours, various shades of green and red being very prettily combined. They are finished off with leather tassels, and look quite smart. Two of these bridles are used for every camel. The one by which they are usually driven goes simply round the neck, and is quite sufficient for ordinary control or guidance ; but the other, which is placed through the fleshy and very tender part of the extremity of the nose, is used in case the camel attempts to run off, or in any way becomes obstreperous, when, unless he gets completely beyond restraint, a sharp pull will reduce him to obedience at once.

But I must return to our start from the birsch village, though you will scarcely believe me when I tell you of what happened on that occasion, and I myself could not understand it until Charlie interpreted it to me afterwards. I was just about to mount "Wad Zaid" when Ahmed came up and said that all the women of the place were very anxious to see me, as they had never beheld a European woman ; but they could not possibly come out to where we were, not only on account of the presence of all the men of the village and of our servants, who were strange to them, but especially because Charlie was there, which in itself would have been reason enough to deter them had we been alone ! I at once consented to go to see them, and was conducted away some distance to a number of bushes which had been trained into a sort of arbour, behind which about twenty of my dark-skinned friends were congregated. They "salaamed," and I returned the greeting, and was endeavouring to commence with a few polite phrases when one of them suddenly advanced and, taking hold of my arm, though not roughly, commenced trying to turn up my sleeve. I was utterly amazed, but before I could find words to express my astonishment or ask an explanation, or even before I could withdraw my arm, a second lady made a dive at my neck and endeavoured to force a gap under the silk handkerchief which I always wore tied closely round my throat. A third simultaneously attacked the buttons of my habit; but *this* was altogether too much. I was perfectly dumbfoundered! Never had anything approaching to rude conduct occurred before, and I was indignant and bewildered. Wrenching myself away with firmness and decision I stood defiant at a little distance, and, pouring forth disapproving negatives, explained that such conduct was not the custom in my country. What altogether perplexed me was that these extraordinary actions appeared in no way to be prompted by any ill feeling, and I immediately became almost sorry—although still lost in amazement—at having shown myself so wrathful. My peculiar acquaintances at once desisted and fell back a little, jabbering vociferously among themselves ; but no further attempt was made to approach me. At that moment, to my great relief, I heard the voice of Ahmed on the other side of the arbour saying that the Khawajah wished to start ; so, bidding a more hasty farewell than I had ever yet taken of any natives, I quickly quitted the group, and took myself and my injured feelings away to the camels.

When we had mounted and were on our way I told Charlie of what had happened ; and he at once elucidated the circumstance by assuring me that they had only wished to discover whether I was white! as all that they could see of me was burned to a hue so very nearly resembling their own that they evidently looked upon the reports that had reached them of fair-skinned women as perfect fabrications, and desired to ascertain the truth for themselves. The explanation, which I found afterwards to be painfully correct, was almost as startling to myself as my appearance had been to these good ladies ;

but as you will remember that my only looking-glass for weeks had been a small pocket pin-cushion, you will scarcely be surprised that this fact was a revelation I was not prepared for.

It was a lovely evening; and as we knew that we could get no more water after leaving that village until we reached the Settit river—a march which would take the baggage camels, at their best pace, nearly seventy-two hours—we knew we should have to go on nearly all night, and to do with as little rest as possible.

On leaving Kassala the Pasha had given us two soldiers as an escort, and one of these men was put in especial charge of the camels carrying the water-skins,—*now* the most precious possession in the caravan. We went on for a good many miles, and the ground was pretty smooth all the way till we came to a little khor, or dry watercourse, which was rough and broken. In descending this the camels got out of their regular line, and, whether by design or inadvertence—strong suspicion pointing to the former—the water-camels got behind, though special orders had been given that they should always remain in the centre of the cavalcade. It had become quite dusk, and the moon was only just rising, when we became aware that they, with several of the camel men and servants, and also the soldier in charge, were far in the background! They had actually halted, opened the skins, and were distributing "stolen water" all round.

This was as flagrant a betrayal of trust as the soldier could have been capable of. He well knew the absolute necessity, for all our sakes, and his own into the bargain, of being provident with that precious liquid. An express command had been given that not a drop was to be taken except under Charlie's supervision, and at stated times, when a proper distribution would be made to all; yet now in the evening, when no one could yet be suffering from the thirst which would be inevitable by day, he had not only permitted the men to take the water but had shared the draughts himself. Instant retribution fell with promptitude upon the guilty party, the "kurbatch" (the buffalo-hide whip of the country) coming swiftly into play, and convincing them speedily of their error, or, at any rate, of the consequences, which they justly deserved, and might expect on a repetition of such offences. You may be shocked to hear it, but I feel convinced that in instances of this sort prompt punishment is the only way in which to deal with these natives. Good qualities they have ; but remonstrance or persuasion in matters of life and death with people as uncontrolled as children, and deceitful both by nature and habit, would be folly ; and one might live to rue the leniency which had been no real kindness. The result, on this occasion, of the admonition was that the evil did not occur again during our waterless marches.

LETTER XX.

HAMZA'S ZAREEBA, 25*th March.*

IT was midnight before we halted after the last march I told you of, and then took place the first authorised distribution of water, for which the self-indulgent men had not waited. All the skins were brought up and placed on matting, just outside the tent, and Charlie presided while it was being doled out. Each man got his share, and the animals had theirs too, after which we ate a hasty cold supper and I went to bed.

You will be surprised at the amount of consecutive marching I did in the next fifty-five hours. Now that it is over I am myself astonished at it, and you must remember that the thermometer (in the shade, of course) was, during that time, at any hour between eight in the morning and five in the evening, never less than 85°, and during the greatest heat of the day often over 100°.

At six o'clock on the morning of the 20th the baggage camels started, but I was literally too tired to move, and craved a little longer rest. Charlie gave me half an hour, and I dared not ask for more ; I knew it was so urgent that we should be off. By seven we were mounted and away, and we were not long in overtaking the caravan. The country was perfectly flat all round, and almost as bare and dusty as a sandy shore.

About eleven o'clock I began to feel the heat so intensely that we determined to go on to a khor, which was only a few miles off, where we hoped to find a few trees, perhaps some palms, and to await there the arrival of the camels. The other soldier who, since the delinquency of the first one, had been given charge over the water was now very seriously harangued, and every camel man and servant was solemnly and threateningly admonished as to his behaviour with regard to the girbas.

We took a few of the servants with us and set off. About noon we reached the khor, which we found to be much smaller than we expected, and to have only a few scraggy bushes in it ; but we made the most of these by putting coverings over the branches for shade, and lay down on our farrwahs. When the others came up they brought with them a woeful proof of the effect of the heat : one of our dogs was dying ; it was the one which had been given me by my kind Italian friend at Kassala, and it had probably never been exposed to so trying a life before.

They had taken the poor thing up, and were carrying it on a camel, and for its sake they had ventured to disobey the mandate regarding the water. For this they were not pardoned but *thanked*, and applauded for their care ; but all efforts to save the poor thing's life proved fruitless. I took her myself under our tree, laid her on some matting in the shade, and gave her " Liebig's extract," which we were never without, and reviving draughts, but all to no purpose—she was too far gone, and in about half an hour, with a few convulsive shudders, she expired. It was a melancholy commencement to the march—about which, on several

accounts, we could not but feel a little anxious—
and did not tend to raise our spirits! Hot as
it was, before four o'clock we started again, but
I soon began to feel terribly exhausted and even
quite faint.

The fact was that, with more zeal perhaps
than discretion, being anxious to take my share
in assisting to economise the water, I had suggested that we should not have anything cooked
during our halt; so we had made shift with
biscuits and other slight fare, and until we began
to march again I had felt quite valiant, but I
now determined not to try that experiment in
future. I procured some more biscuits from the
lunch-basket, and with these and something
else, of which a Good Templar would disap-
prove, I managed to revive, though at one time
I really feared I should have had to bring our
whole party to a stop, which would have been
the most unfortunate circumstance that could
possibly have happened.

We went on till about eleven o'clock, when
we came unexpectedly upon a very large caravan, which was halting under some sickly-look-
ing trees in the open plain. We soon saw that
there were animals of all kinds in the midst
of a sort of enclosure, formed by baggage, and

branches that had been hastily cut, and a nearer inspection showed us numbers of swarthy forms moving about, evidently in possession.

We immediately guessed that this was a menagerie—or, at any rate, a collection of wild beasts intended for a menagerie—on its way home to Europe, and this proved to be the case. They were bound for Hanover, and the German gentleman who was in charge was smoking a cigarette under a tree, having just finished his dinner. His servants, Arabs of course, immediately ran off to tell him that European travellers were on the road, and he quickly came forward and most kindly begged us to dismount and rest for a while. We gladly accepted his invitation, and were soon in the midst of a genial circle, with one or two other Europeans besides himself, chatting of the perils of the way and drinking coffee.

It was *so* pleasant to meet these members of a civilised land in the midst of that cheerless march, and they seemed almost fellow-countrymen at once in contrast to the darkies all around, who at once appeared to become more completely foreign and alien than they had been before! In half an hour's time, however, we felt that we must be on again, as the night was too fine and clear to lose, and the baggage camels had gone ahead while we were halting.

The astonishment of the Arab servants belonging to this caravan at my riding a camel —and such an immense one too—was very great; their exclamations of surprise were undisguised; and when, on leaving the camp, we trotted off at a smart pace, a chorus of amazement broke forth, which the distinct repetition of the word "sitt" (lady) caused me to appropriate in my own favour.

At half-past one we halted, but for four hours only; and then Charlie insisted on my having a good supper. During the morning's march he had been fortunate in getting several Guinea fowl, and these were now most acceptable. We did not have a tent pitched, but, as I have done before, I lay down in my travelling dress on a rug, and in that position got a little rest.

Soon after five we were on our camels again, and with only two hours' interval—once about ten o'clock in the morning, and again about four in the afternoon—we journeyed the whole day, and no words can possibly describe the pain and fatigue of that journey of the 21st of March. There is nothing to tell about it except that we

went on, and on, and on, and felt that there
was nothing to be done but to go on and get
over it as soon as we could.   Three of the dogs
had to be carried on camels, and we stopped
more than once to give them water; but in the
evening poor Shot, the pointer, died; like the
former one, he had been simply killed by the
heat.   That night I was obliged to halt and
have a little rest, or I verily believe I should
have died too! for we had been marching for
seventeen hours and a half, with only two inter-
mediate rests of an hour at a time, and, in addition, three short halts of about twenty minutes
each, when we had strong coffee and were off
again.   We stopped at 11 P.M., had a small
tent pitched, and did not go on till six in the
morning.   For the first part of the march everything was just a repetition of the previous days,
but about ten o'clock the heat became so unbearable that every dog except Debûs began
to droop, and we thought we should scarcely
get one of them in alive; we have still six, for
the original number had increased to eight.

They were all taken up, and we made a con-
trivance for carrying them, which was the best
we could devise.   This was done by placing
them inside large nets, which are made to go

over the girbas.   Out of these nets temporary
hammocks were constructed, in each of which
a dog was placed, and they were then slung to
the camel-saddles.   They were fastened high
up, and indeed partly rested on the camels'
backs, so that there was no swinging motion
that could be disturbing; but in spite of these
precautions nothing would induce some of the
dogs to approve of their new resting-places,
and such plungings and struggles ensued that
in the case of two of them we feared they would
tear the nets to pieces, and might be killed by
falling out of them; so there was nothing to be
done but to take them out, and for the servants
who were riding to carry them as best they
could.   Several times we stopped to give them
water, but the poor things actually could not
drink! and this, added to the fact that the
supply of water was getting short, created an
aspect that began altogether to make us feel
somewhat uneasy at the general condition of
things.   This culminated when the new camel
drivers, whom we had brought from Kassala,
now began to disagree among themselves as to
the shortest route to the Settit.

At this most disconcerting moment, in the
midst of our dire perplexity, we happened, by

great good luck, to meet a small caravan coming
north. The Arabs who were with it put us
upon the right track, and also spared us a little
water; and better than all, one of them, who
seemed to have no particular object in the
direction he was travelling in, volunteered to
turn back and show us the way. He pointed
out the route he would take, and as, by the
compass which we always carried, it had every
appearance of being the shortest and best road,
we decided to follow it.

I had felt the heat and fatigue so much that
morning that no position seemed endurable for
long, and I had quite sympathised with the
poor dogs when they did not like the hammocks.
I had started on my camel, but after a few
miles changed to the donkey, then back again
to the camel, and again to the donkey, and I
was on " Prince " when we had met this caravan,
and had decided, after a little consultation, to
take the new volunteer as our guide.

He was one of the " Tukruri " tribe, who
are chiefly negroes inhabiting a tract of country
south of the Settit, for the most part between
the Atbara or Black Nile and the borders of
Abyssinia; so as, in returning, he would be
going in the direction of his own country, we

thought we might trust him! and we were not deceived ; we engaged his services, and started. It was then about noon, and Charlie proposed that, as the heat had become so intense, we should leave the baggage camels and go on ahead as quickly as we could with the Tukruri man. I gladly acquiesced, deserted "Prince" for " Wad Zaid," and after complete directions had been given to the drivers as to the course we intended to pursue, and they had been repeatedly charged to follow in our wake, we set off.

The Tukruri was a strong-looking fellow, with a sort of bull-dog, determined face, and went straight ahead at once, without a moment's hesitation as to the way. He was rather a short thick-set man, but he carried a very long spear, which gave him in a measure an appearance of height. He wore no covering on his black woolly head, and he had a loose flowing garment, which, in spite of his running, never seemed to be girded round him or tucked away, as most Arabs twist up their clothes when moving quickly, so that he was quite unlike any former guide we had had ; and I shall never forget the comical appearance he presented as he jogged along before us at a regular sort of steady trot. After we had been a short time on the road we got into a bit of jungle between some hills, in which, among palms, and even tamarisks, there were the unceasing thorny mimosas. The garment of our guide still flew hither and thither as he ran, and it was a matter of the greatest marvel to me that it was not continually caught by the thorns ; I expected momently to see him brought up short by a sudden tug, but a dexterous twitch just at the right moment saved him over and over again, and I believe that in the end that cotton sheet never so much as brushed against a bush.

We went on at a good pace until we got to some rising ground, from near which Charlie said he was sure we should be able to see the mountains of Abyssinia. He was so anxious to show these to me that, in spite of our haste, we made a little divergence to the right, mounted a bit of ground still higher, and from there distinctly saw, about fifty miles distant, an irregular blue line against the sky, which are the mountains close to the spot at which the river Takazze enters Abyssinia. I earnestly hope that some day I may cross those mountains and find myself in King John's country, for I should dearly like to go into the land of which I have already heard so much.

After about two minutes, or not so long, on this higher ground, we descended again, and continued to press on for the river. For a considerable time travelling became even more painful and troublesome than before; the mimosas were so numerous that it was quite difficult to get along; there was no track already made, and we had to wedge our way in and out among the bushes, avoiding the thorns as best we could. The dry hot wind burned us most painfully, but the scorching of the sun was still worse! and it needed all the resolution one could summon to keep up, for this trying march came at the end of three days' exhaustion, and this it was that caused me to feel it so acutely. At length, about 2 P.M., with joy unspeakable, from the edge of the high plateau we had been traversing for more than two hours previously, we suddenly looked down upon the longed-for Settit.

It lay below us in the valley, a bright glittering sheet of water, its bright surface sparkling like millions of diamonds in the dazzling light. For a moment I could scarcely believe, in spite of my hopes and wishes, that it might not be a mirage again! It seemed too good to be true, that we had really reached the water; but it *was* true, there was no doubt about it, and we felt with inexpressible gratitude that our fatigues and difficulties were at an end.

We took a road which led us to an Arab village close by, and as we passed through the narrow lanes and paths among the houses, the villagers ceased their occupations and gazed at us with amazement, and the children fled in every direction, shrieking and vociferating in shrill tones, to make known to others the strange apparitions that had suddenly dropped into their midst !

By the time we had got to the rest-house, as usual a birsch hut, all were either gathering courage or congregating together for the general defence, and a goodly multitude was assembled *en masse* to watch us dismount ; and the chief of the tribe, who had his residence in the village, immediately came forward to disarm the fears of his people and to give us welcome. He was quite a youth, only about nineteen, and seemed to have a quiet dignity of manner that would have been most imposing had I not soon discovered it to be due to dense stupidity ! He had nothing either to ask or say, and absolute silence soon ensued, nobody appearing to be even half as intelligent as our

negro friends of long ago at Lagua! He sat
down, however, in the rest-house, surrounded
by his special suite; and an indiscriminate

THE YOUTHFUL CHIEF.

multitude in addition, as usual, darkened the
doorway.

I found a kind of rough and rustic couch in
one corner, made of cross bars of unhewn wood,
and on this, with the usual trappings from the
camels, was only too glad to rest. I should

have been so thankful to have been left alone, but this was totally impossible, the gaze of the multitude had to be endured for a time at any rate; and the very fact of at least forty pairs of eyes staring full at one, in the midst of grim silence, was, in spite of its possessing a decided element of the comical, almost enough to bring one to one's last gasp.   Very shortly some delicious water, slightly flavoured, as on former occasions, with honey, was brought to us in gourds, and I was so completely parched and burned that my thirst seemed unquenchable. I drank untold quantities, and it was only a sense of prudence in the end—not from feeling satisfied!—that I stopped at last.

After about an hour the Arab sheik, who was a polite but, as I have said, a dull boy, took his leave, the multitude went with him, and our longed-for solitude came at last.   I was too worn out to do anything but shut my eyes and try to sleep; the hut was happily very dark, and this was an unspeakable comfort.   I was resting and half dozing, and at last I began to feel, in addition to fatigue, that I was famishing, as it was then nearly three o'clock, and, except coffee and biscuits during one short halt, we had had nothing substantial since half-past five that morning. The baggage camels, however, had not yet come up, and until they appeared we saw no chance of getting anything to eat. We were rather bemoaning our fate, when these kindly and thoughtful native people came to the rescue, as at other times their countrymen had done before them. A gentle voice seeking admittance was unexpectedly heard outside, and very quietly and slowly the piece of matting that formed the entrance to the hut was raised, when a servant belonging to the sheik appeared, bringing a large wooden tray, on which was a wooden bowl, containing a stewed fowl, some round cakes made of durra—extremely like oaten cakes, not at all a bad substitute for bread—and a little saucepan full of hot coffee. More than acceptable was the repast, and on *this* occasion the absence of knives and forks formed no barrier to my full appreciation of the friendly gift. Like my hostesses at Kassala I now fully realised the force of the proverb that "fingers were made before forks," and I assure you not even the rich gravy, in which the fowl was swimming, deterred me from dipping into the dish ; indeed, I think it but added zest, for in itself it was excellently flavoured, and I was literally too tired and hungry to care in what manner I obtained food so long as I got it.

In the course of the afternoon the baggage and servants arrived, and about half-past five we again mounted our camels, said good-bye to the young chief, to whose hospitality we were so greatly indebted, and moved to a large zareeba about two miles away, which belonged to the German merchant whom we had known so well at Kassala, but the Arab superintendent of which is named " Hamza"; and so the zareeba is always known as " Hamza's zareeba." It is this place I am now writing from. We have a straw hut in the midst of the compound, and as it is a very large enclosure there is plenty of room for all the camels and servants too. By and by, too, we shall very likely have our tents pitched, for we shall perhaps be here some little time, forming our plans for the coming sport, as we have at last reached the land of big game.

LETTER XXI.

EL GWAIYA, 3d *April.*

A LONG gap has occurred since my last, and I
fear I have lost or shall lose a couple of mails ;
but the fact is I have been ill and unable to
write. That march across the waterless desert
had its revenge and took it out of me afterwards ; and even, though I am very much
better now, I am not yet quite up to the mark.
This is most provoking, as it is hindering and
even threatening to upset our plans ; and at
present it is stopping Charlie's shooting, for he
does not like to leave me until I am all right
again.

When we moved away from the birsch
hut, which had been our first resting-place on

the Settit, and went over to the zareeba from which I last wrote, I had felt much revived and that night slept well; but it was the last good sleep I have had since then. Next day I was very feverish and scarcely fit for anything, and have not been much better (with a very bad bit in the interval) until the present time.

The fact is, I took a chill from drinking the " honey water," which was so irresistible, too soon after the long hot march; and this chill brought on fever. I thought that the water could not be harmful as it had been just slightly warmed; this was done in the most delicate manner possible, not so much as to prevent it from being refreshing, but merely enough to take off the extreme cold, which is the thing to be dreaded.

The Arabs are aware of this, and will not themselves run the risk of drinking pure cold water immediately after severe exercise; but in this instance I was too absolutely burned to have made it safe to drink anything at all for a good time, and ought not to have done it. If we had needed an additional proof to that which our own feelings had given us of the intense heat of that march, we had it in the way the poor dogs suffered.

When the caravan came in we found that not only had a third died on the road, but that the servants had had the greatest difficulty in saving some of the others, and for a long time we were really very doubtful whether we should not lose two more. Elfie and Fairy were still living, but I never saw anything so terribly distressing as the condition of their poor backs. I scarcely like to tell you about them. They were so literally *scorched* that the skin had entirely come off, and left simply a strip of raw bleeding sore from their shoulders to their tails; but the invaluable " neat's-foot oil," which I had previously found so good for my own face, was at once carefully applied, and with its wonderfully healing power very soon effected a cure. They are now almost well ; and, as they are kept carefully in the shade all day, I trust that before we have a long march again the poor creatures will be quite " themselves again."

I ought to have told you ere this that in coming to the Settit we are in the country of the Hamran Arabs—the people who hunt and kill all their big game (principally elephants) with swords. These are their only weapons, and the tribe is known as the "sword-hunters." It is a most dangerous method of sport, and they constantly

run the greatest risks, but their clever strata-
gems and long practice almost always ensure
success, and accidents are very rare.   They
proceed in the following manner.

SWORD-HUNTERS.

Never less than three men attack an elephant
at a time, and they take care to select one
which happens to be by itself—apart from a
herd.   Having penetrated into the depths of
the jungle, where during the greatest heat of

the day the elephants retreat for shade and
sleep, they rouse their intended victim by
shouts and vociferations, until from provocation
it rises in pursuit. One of the Arabs then, as
by previous arrangement, turns as a decoy and
runs. The elephant follows him, but the man
being swift of foot and able to turn much more
quickly, and in a smaller space than the immense four-footed beast, wheels quickly round
and escapes. He repeats this manœuvre several
times, and the elephant, with each turn becoming more and more enraged, and intent only on
following the man, loses sight of everything
else. Meanwhile, the other two Arabs, as agile
as their companion, and wholly unobserved by
their foe, rush up behind, and by swift unerring
strokes from their sharp swords rapidly ham-
string him, when he immediately falls over and
becomes an easy prey.

Hamza's zareeba, from which my last two
letters were written, had a large share of it dedicated to young wild beasts, that were, after being
somewhat tamed and more fully grown, to go to
Kassala, preparatory to being sent to Europe
with those that we had already seen there.

There were tiny giraffes, a small specimen
of the river-horse discovered by Sir Samuel

Baker, a couple of young hyenas, little monkeys of rare sorts, wild pigs, and many other kinds; this was in fact a sort of nursery depôt for the larger collection. We often used to visit these young curiosities and to watch them getting their milk, especially in the mornings and evenings when it was cool, and we left our hut. A large herd of goats was kept specially for the benefit of these infants, and immense gourds, full of lovely milk topped with rich froth, were brought in for them three times a day.

This enclosure was so very unlike any other that we have hitherto stopped in, or any of the camping-grounds that we have come to, that I must describe it, and then you will be able to realise what a zareeba on the bank of an African river is really like.

Near these banks, trees and shrubs of many kinds often grow pretty thickly for some distance inland, and it was so at this part of the Settit, this particular spot having the additional advantage of being close by a place which makes a good ford when the water is low; and on this account, as well as from the thickness of the jungle, it had been selected for a zareeba. A broad space, over an acre in extent, had been cut away, and the thorny branches had been taken to make not only the outer wall, but the barriers inside it, which divide the various spaces appropriated to different purposes.

The whole place was very picturesque,— almost every nook of it would have made a pretty sketch; and this was especially the case in the evenings, when the camels and goats, which had been outside grazing off such bushes and herbage as they could find, were brought in, and their feeds of durra were served out to them.

To the left, as you entered, the camel men had taken up their station; they seemed to appreciate deep shade after all! for they appropriated a couple of very large trees, and a little thicket beyond it, in which shady bowers had been cleverly formed by clearing out all the tangled thorny branches underneath, and leaving thick arches of interlaced twigs, interspersed with occasional patches of green, overhead. I think they made these their sleeping-places, for I used to see mats and rough bits of sacking peeping out here and there from snug corners; and their cooking evidently went on under the trees, for blue smoke wreathed up under them in the mornings and evenings at the time that savoury scents filled the atmosphere.

I was rejoiced to see that a good deal of laundry work evidently went on among the natives during this halt; they seemed to be taking advantage of the river, for I used to behold numerous clothes spread out over the tops of the bowers to dry, and the garments that were donned after we had been there a few days had decidedly a whiter hue than any that had appeared while we were on the road. The baggage camels were beyond, behind our dromedaries, which had a separate little enclosure to themselves, though all were safely within the thorny hedge. Farther away than the camels came the goats, in a division by themselves; and coming round again towards our hut, but behind it, were the kitchen and our servants' quarters.

A long shed, running round a part of the zareeba, had been given up for this double purpose, and, as they had also the shelter of several small trees and shrubs, the servants were in clover. In the centre of the ground was the straw hut which we occupied, and which, though spacious enough, and no doubt at one time very substantial, was then more picturesque than perfect, the flat roof being full of chinks and holes, which, though principally at the corners, rendered it insufficient to keep out the intense heat.

In a more remote division still, but facing us, was the nursery-ground of the young animals I have mentioned, so you see that an acre, wide as it is, would easily be covered by all the various inmates, biped and quadruped, that I have intimated ; and, with variations according to the requirements of such an encampment, I think Hamza's zareeba may be taken as a fair specimen of the African encampment known by that name.

The morning after our arrival we were startled at early dawn by a tremendous noise, like the rushing of a great wind or the sudden rising of mighty flames, and started up, expecting to see the jungle on fire, and to find that we were in jeopardy of being "burnt out."

To our unutterable surprise all this commotion was caused by tiny birds flying in dense masses—millions of them, I am sure, there must have been—out of all the neighbouring bushes and shrubs.

The same thing occurred regularly, day after day, at the same hour. These minute feathered things, as small as humming-birds, and far smaller than many Eastern butterflies, came

home at night to roost, and were off again, no
one knew whither, with the first ray of daylight,
and, though each was too diminutive to have
made any audible sound by itself, the combined
movement of the multitude was as tremendous
as I have described it. The female of these
birds was brown, the male principally a dullish
red, and they were not in either case remarkable
for beauty.

After several days at this spot, finding I was
not likely to be able to move for some time, the
large Indian tent that we had brought from
Penang was put up, which, with its double roof
and walls, proved, with the additional shade of
a great tree under which it was pitched, much
cooler than the hut, and during the day I was
moved into it. Very often at night, feeling
that both hut and tent were too suffocating to
remain in, I used to have my bedstead moved
outside, and lie gasping for air, and fanning
myself almost till the morning.

I shall never forget the night of the 27th.
I had not been able to stir from my angréb in
the hut all day, for the fever had been at its
height, and when evening came, exhausted as I
was, it had not passed off sufficiently for me to
get any sleep. I lay parched and faint, while

Charlie tried every sort of restorative, none having effect for long, and at last what do you think he resorted to? Although I had always hitherto despised it, he tried mesmerism! and actually mesmerised me into a happy stupor, from which I ultimately sank to sleep. It was the first time I had ever yielded to this influence, and I really think it proved a turning-point in my illness, for, though the fever is intermittent, and often provokingly comes back when I think I have got rid of it for good and all, it was not so bad for several days after that night as it had been before.

There was an enormous tree, the biggest of all in the compound, just outside our hut; alas! it was almost leafless, but the branches were so thick that they afforded a sort of shelter from the sun, and under their protection Charlie used to hold quite a little court! It is wonderful how quickly the news of any traveller's arrival spreads through the land. Chiefs from all the districts round, far and wide, heard that he was wishing to shoot, and making inquiries about the country and game, and came flocking in to give him advice. Of course the particular counsel of each separate chief was that the only part of the whole " Hamran " which combined every advantage, and would suit his exact purpose, was the individual tract occupied by the individual speaker, and that he would make an irretrievable mistake in going any- where else!

This repeated assurance threatened to render the advice of each utterly useless, and to sift the facts down to the truth seemed almost hopeless, especially as we knew that it is acknowledged by the natives as a decided advantage to them to have Europeans in their neighbourhood.

We were, however, immensely assisted in our perplexity by unexpectedly hearing that only about three miles off were two German gentlemen, who were also engaged in buying and collecting wild animals for a menagerie in Europe; and a few days after our halt one of them came over to see us. He was, fortunately for me, a doctor; and when he heard I was ill, begged to be allowed to prescribe for me at once.

The presence of this physician in a remote district of the far-off Soudan was another of those wonderful pieces of good luck which con- tinually occurred to us during our travel; and I shall always feel that I was indebted to his kind care for my comparatively easy recovery. The first visit paid us by Dr. Bijorath (for that was his name) was at the commencement slightly embarrassing, from our mutual want of a language in common. The doctor spoke only German, which neither Charlie nor myself know much of ; and for the first half-hour it was rather uphill work.

I did not attempt to assist, feeling sure I should do anything but *that!* but mischievously watched the struggles of the others with silent amusement ; and, "though I say it that shouldn't," I never had a more astonishing proof of Charlie's aptitude for rapidly acquiring a language than on that occasion. It is a positive fact that before an hour had elapsed he was conversing with our new friend with the greatest ease, and now, at the end of another week, he holds long conversations on all kinds of intricate subjects, entirely in German, with both him and Herr Löhse (the other gentleman to whom I before referred).

They talk politics, and discuss governments and literature, and hold even theological discussions ! the various points of which are translated to me afterwards. These gentlemen have shown us such immense kindness that I feel we can never be grateful enough to them; and, indeed, it is in their zareeba that we are now located.

Directly Dr. Bijorath found that I had fever he urged us most strongly to leave Hamza's zareeba — which is in rather a low situation, close to the bank of the river—and to come over to the other side, on which they were encamped, where the ground is much higher and more open, and the air purer. We did not, however, move the next day, as he was anxious we should do ; and very soon he was back again, accompanied by several Arabs, bringing all kinds of good things for us, among them fresh vegetables from a garden they keep well watered and tended with much care, on a little strip of land close beside the river-bank — lettuce, cucumbers, and turnips growing to perfection ; and he also brought an urgent message from Herr Löhse, joined to fresh persuasions of his own, that we would not delay to move our camp. At last it was finally settled that we should do so, and on the morning of the 31st, as I thought I could then manage it, I once more mounted my dear "Wad Zaid," and we crossed the river.

We got off by half-past six, and, leaving the

camels to follow, were conducted by some Arabs who knew the way to the zareeba of our friends, which was not above an hour's ride distant, even taking it slowly. The country was the prettiest we had yet come through, either before reaching Kassala or since leaving it. The ground all the way was much higher and far more undulating than before, and, as the river wound about a good deal, was well wooded; for, wherever there is water, trees will always grow. Everything now is, of course, very far from verdant, but I can well believe that here, after the rains, the whole land would be lovely. We crossed the river twice on our march, and to reach Herr Löhse's camp we had to ascend a very steep path from the last ford to the top of the high plateau on which he has wisely located himself.

On attaining this summit we found both gentlemen kindly waiting to welcome us; and the warm, genial greeting we received made me feel almost perfectly well at once. We were, however, overwhelmed to find that they had actually vacated their own well-built grass houses in our behalf, and had taken up their abode in a long shed in the background which had formerly been used for some of the animals.

Such extreme kindness on the part of complete strangers was quite overpowering ; we had merely intended to have our own tents pitched in a favourable spot near their encampment, and then perhaps to have some grass or straw huts erected, as we thought that in all probability we should find even the Indian tent too thin for the daily increasing heat. Now, however, quite a suite of apartments was at our disposal. The huts have been beautifully made ; they are extremely thick, so that the sun has not the remotest chance of inserting even the tiniest ray at any time, and they are, in consequence, delightfully cool all day long, as, to begin with, they never become heated.

Outside our rooms there is a large verandah, which, having a roof, forms quite a room in itself; and here we take early coffee in the mornings, and sit chatting in the evenings with our friends when their daily labours are over.

This verandah is open at the sides, and, as it faces the whole zareeba, we have most amusing views from it of all that goes on. There is a much larger collection of animals here than there was at Hamza's, and five young elephants and two baby hippopotami are rich subjects for laughter and mirth ; but I will come to them in

course of time. Herr Löhse is the head of
this camp, the one who is in charge,— Dr.
Bijorath having accompanied him merely out
of friendship.

He is very young to be in so responsible a
position, being only about twenty-six, but he
has already been employed for several years by
the same firm at Hamburg, and is thoroughly
well fitted for the work ; and he is so very
charming that I must describe him. He is
very tall, and being about six feet two in height,
has an erect manly carriage, and is decidedly
handsome, with a frank expression that is full
of humour looking out of a pair of deep-blue
eyes. Having plenty of character, decision,
and energy (at the same time that he is perfectly gentle and refined), he is quite up to these
natives, who are seldom or ever able to find a
weak point in him ; yet he is full of kindness,
and has a wonderful way of managing them.

He personally superintends everything in
his zareeba, and his days are thoroughly occupied. He does not himself go out to get
animals, but buys those which the Arabs bring
in ; and practice has made him as keen a critic
as to the "points" of a youthful hippo, lion,
leopard, elephant, or whatever the specimen

for sale may be, as an English sportsman is as to the merits, or the reverse, of a horse or hound.

He enjoys the free, wild life of the desert thoroughly ; but in the evening, when the day's work has come to an end, he takes his concertina—the loved companion of all his travels —and plays (with the tenderness and beautiful expression that a sensitive nature only is capable of) the most exquisite melodies from all the best operas, filling the air with delicious music. I cannot tell you how I look forward to these sweet evening hours : the whole scene is then perfect, and, like a hundred other scenes of our daily life, totally unlike anything that could be experienced in any other country.

LETTER XXII.

Our friends have gone !—Difficulty of taking animals to Europe
——Breaking in elephants—The steep descent—Herr
Löhse's courage—On the shore at last—The baby hippos
—Boxes made for them—Goats taken for milk—Baths
for hippos—Stratagem—Distrust awakened—Captured
at last—Slung between camels—Farewell—" Auf wiedersehen "—We miss the concertina.

EL GWAIYA, 8*th April*.

ALAS ! since I last wrote to you we have lost our
kind friends, and I cannot tell you how greatly
we miss them. They left at the beginning of
the week, and Herr Löhse said he feared he
had delayed too long already, for every day
later, at this season of the year, considerably
increases the fatigues and difficulties of the
journey, and renders it additionally doubtful as
to whether all the animals that are going to
Europe will ever arrive there. Numbers often
expire on the way, and even after having
reached the sea-coast they sometimes, in spite
of all the care that is taken of them, die on
board ship, probably the result of the previous

exhaustion of the march. It is very provoking
that some of the most valuable animals are the
least likely to survive—hippos, for instance,
often die *en route*. You would scarcely believe
that a great rough creature like a hippopotamus
is delicate, or that it could suffer much. Yet in
a state of captivity they do not always prove to
be strong animals, and the privations they are
obliged to endure on a march are often very
great.

It is extremely difficult to supply them with
their daily bath, without which they languish
terribly, and young hippos require immense
quantities of milk, which in the hot weather is
scarce, the people themselves being very reluctant to part with it. The restraint, too, and the
fettered conditions so contrary to their nature,
tell upon them, so that one way and another
the homeward route is a trying time for them,
and an anxious· one for their owners. The
latter often suffer much in a pecuniary way
from these losses ; for not only is the outlay in
buying the animals considerable, but great
expense is also incurred in rearing them, until
they are old enough to travel ; and the vexation,
too, which is caused by their deaths, after all
the time and trouble that have been expended

on them is most disheartening. For a fortnight before they started on the journey Herr
Löhse used to take out his young elephants
daily for a morning walk, for the sole purpose
of teaching them how they were to behave on
the march.

This was almost the first and certainly the
principal step towards breaking them in, and
the process was very amusing and really a little
alarming! I shall never forget the scene the
first time I witnessed it. It was the morning
after our arrival; we were having coffee in the
verandah preparatory to going out ourselves,
for, though still far from well, I thought I
could manage a short turn while it was cool,
when the novel procession suddenly emerged
from the elephant-shed at the farther end of
the encampment. The young pedestrians were
about half-grown, not *baby* elephants by any
means, and consequently no joke to deal with.
They appeared to be in the most frisky and
excited condition possible on that particular
morning, though I was told that they were
then quite "tame," compared to what they had
been at first. They were all strongly chained
together one behind the other, with five Arabs
surrounding each one, all endeavouring to act

as conductors and restrainers to the especial
youngster under their charge ; yet, in spite of
these guides, the wild dashes that the whole
gang constantly made in forbidden directions
were quite terrifying, and I began seriously to
apprehend that as they had to pass close to us
they might even knock down the poles of the
verandah, and sweep it away wherever their
fancies for the moment dictated !

It was difficult to imagine what they must
have been when they were *less* " tame." They
came rolling and tumbling along, curling their
long trunks about, and shuffling their great flat
feet deep into the dust, of which they kicked up
such clouds that sometimes we could scarcely
see them, and were ourselves almost suffocated.
As they drew near I observed that in the case
of each elephant one of the five Arabs in
attendance on him held a strong rope fastened
securely round his near front leg, another a
similar rope attached to his off hind, while a
third man walked at his head leading him, and
a fourth followed behind to remind him at
rebellious moments of the duty of advancing !
—the fifth Arab accompanied the party to give
extra help if needed in any emergency. As
there were five elephants there were altogether

twenty-five Arabs with them, besides a vast and motley crowd of stray onlookers; and Herr Löhse himself was there too, marching at the head of the cavalcade, hunting-whip in hand, and, in spite of his quiet appearance, seeming to be everywhere and to see everything at once. Close by the houses, which had been kindly appropriated to our use, was the steep path which we had ascended on coming up to the zareeba, and after getting by us, at which time they chanced, to my great relief, to be particularly quiet and well behaved, the elephants had to go down this path to the plain below, on which they were to be exercised.

They were led out by this particular route every morning in order that when the time arrived for their final departure they should go to it naturally and as a familiar way. As yet, however, they had not become quite so accustomed to it as was desired, and, as there was a precipice on one side and the path itself was none too wide, their evident dislike to descend it was somewhat justifiable, and it certainly was an ugly place for any unsteady conduct.

I went to the top to watch them go down, and, to use a vulgar phrase, my " heart leapt to my mouth" more than once before they were all safely landed at the bottom. On the very summit they came, as if by general consent, to a dead stop, and looked the very impersonation of obstinacy; nothing would induce them to stir, and both Herr Löhse and the servants were reluctant to force them lest, if they became angry or frightened, a sudden rush should precipitate, not only themselves but their attendants also over the edge of the ravine.

Coaxing words, gentle pats, and persuasive tones were used, but all in vain. I was told that they had never been so determined not to move as they seemed that morning; and it really appeared that they must have got up the little drama for my especial benefit! But they had to be conquered; if kindness did not succeed, other measures must be taken; one thing alone was certain, they must not, either on this or on any other occasion, be allowed to remain masters in the field. A few additional Arabs were adroitly slipped in by the side of those already holding the ropes, to grasp them also, and then Herr Löhse's terrific whip was cracked in the air with a report louder than that of a pistol.

An effect was instantly produced, though not exactly the one that was desired. The sound was evidently known and feared, for immediately every trunk was curled up, always a sign of anger, while every head was tossed aloft, and that harsh trumpeting screech which an elephant always emits when frightened was the simultaneous result from the whole number. One or two even raised their trunks and brought them down again with a bang on the ground, producing a hollow reverberating noise like striking an empty beer-barrel, which is another indication on the part of an elephant of terror and displeasure. Still they did not stir, and at last the lash had to be brought sharply down on the back of the leader.

The excitement was at this moment intense, and we all watched breathlessly, for the rush which had been dreaded actually came; but Herr Löhse's wonderful pluck averted all evil consequences. He had stationed himself on the side of the path nearest to the precipice, and by repeated cracks of the whip, and by constantly throwing up his arms, he kept the gang from the edge until they reached the river-bed. Midway they had come to another halt, which from its position threatened to be even more

dangerous than the first; but the difficulty was
sooner surmounted, and after a few ineffectual
struggles to turn back, finding remonstrance
useless, they hurried along to the foot. They
were then taken out for about two miles before
turning to come home.

We soon lost sight of them, for they rattled
along at a great pace and got round a corner;
but Dr. Bijorath afterwards gave us an amusing
description of how they had tried to pull up
every little bush they could get within reach of,
or to stop and rub themselves against every tree
they passed, and that to run away in quite the
opposite direction from that in which they were
designed to go had seemed to be their chief
bent! He assured us, however, that they were
"improving daily"; and certainly on the morning that they started for Kassala they walked
away in an orderly manner that was quite surprising, and even descended the steep path I
have described with little, if any, apparent
reluctance.

The two young hippos that I spoke of before
had also been special objects of interest to me
all the time they were here. Their nursery
happened to be just at the back of our rooms,
but they were kept in such perfect order that

this never troubled us in the least ; and I could hear them splashing in and out of their bath all day long, grunting and snorting now and then, and raising their voices in all sorts of extra-ordinary tones, which I supposed were to be understood as hippo " baby-talk." Getting these infants home was a matter of almost graver anxiety than taking all the rest of his flock. They were very fine young specimens, about the height of a well-grown calf, and had been nourished up for many months previously with the greatest care, the fact of having lost his only hippopotamus on the journey the year before redoubling Herr Löhse's desire to con-vey these safely without a similar *contretemps*. It was decided that they could not walk ; the fatigue would have been far too great, and their slow lumbering pace would have delayed the caravan interminably, so strong wooden boxes were made in which to carry them, innumer-able holes being bored in these to admit air. The first idea was to have bars like those in a hencoop ; but this was rejected, being con-sidered to possess weak points, and solid boxes were determined on instead, the only question that then remained being the best method of how, when the time came, to allure their in-

tended young occupants into them.[1] The
boxes for the hippos were made at Kassala by
the Scotchman I have mentioned, who had a
sawmill there, and sent all the way down to
the Settit river when they were finished; for,
though the Arabs are clever enough as to
knocking up rough sheds or saddles for the
baggage camels, and such things as need only
crude handiwork, they could not have managed
articles like these requiring well-planed, dove-
tailed planks, gigantic clamps, and many devices
to prevent their strange contents from being
able to force their way out at any unexpected
moment; but the fact of these cages having
had to be made at such a distance—for Kassala is nearly a hundred miles from El Gwaiya
—added another to the many minor difficulties
which this laborious life brings with it. The
two most serious considerations of all were how
to supply sufficient water, not only for drinking,
for all this little army of men and animals, but
for the said baths for these same precious hippo-

---

[1] In rewriting my original letter about this I am forcibly
reminded of "Jumbo's" box, and the many difficulties that
were experienced on that memorable occasion before the
sagacious old friend of the "Zoo" was finally enticed into
the enclosure he at first regarded with so much distrust.

potami, and how to obtain milk enough on the road, this being almost the only nourishment that they and many other of the young animals in the collection were able to take. The latter difficulty was partly surmounted by a large flock of goats, which marched with the cavalcade for this sole purpose. It was impossible, however, to take a sufficient number to allow each one of those fed with milk to have the same quantity that they got while in camp, for the very addition of these goats caused the necessity for extra loads of durra to be taken, the whole country being now too completely withered for any animals to be dependent on the herbage they could find. Altogether the commissariat department was, I assure you, a most serious question, and the preparations for it gave me some faint idea of what such an undertaking must be when there is a large campaign to be provided for. There were twenty-five camels for water alone, and ten for durra, yet this was only until they reached Kassala, when the numbers would be considerably increased for the much longer march to Suakin; and the caravan comprised between fifty and sixty animals (besides the transport camels and the goats), nearly forty Arabs to take care of the animals, and last, not least, the two Europeans, with their own personal attendants and their dromedaries and baggage camels.

The question of the mighty baths was so frequent a subject of discussion that it suddenly occurred to us that it might perhaps somewhat solve the difficulty by assisting to economise the water if we presented them with a very thick large waterproof sheet that we happened to have,—one that was designed for making either into a temporary tent, by fixing upright poles into the corners, or for merely using on the ground to keep out damp. It was proposed that after the daily pit had been dug, and before it was filled, this sheet should be laid down and firmly fastened at the corners, which would prevent the water, on being poured on to it, from sinking into the earth and becoming lost. The scheme was considered feasible, and the sheet was accordingly dedicated to these invaluable infants; and we only wished that it had been in our power to contribute in other ways, however small, to the assistance of our never-to-be-forgotten friends, who had done so much for us, and whose kind aid in our time of trouble had been so welcome. And now for the manner in which these young monsters were conveyed into their carriages on the evening of the start. Every sort of inducement was tried in vain, but no amount of coaxing succeeded, and at last force had to be used, though this was done without their being hurt at all. The boxes were brought down to the side of the bath, from which they seemed resolved not to exit, and placed on the brink ; large pails of milk were then put temptingly within the edge of each, and the men who had always brought them their food stood by, using the most persuasive tones they knew to induce their young charges to come up to them.

The stratagem appeared at first likely to succeed, slow and hesitating steps forward being made in response. All was going well, and the difficulty seemed in a fair way of being surmounted, when some chance unlucky movement on the part of one of the Arabs evidently aroused the suspicion of the hippos, and awakened distrust which was never afterwards allayed. Both pairs of small bright eyes twinkled for a moment swiftly and uneasily all round, and with a disapproving snort, half defiant and half frightened, they "slithered" with a tremendous splash back again into the protecting pool. This was terribly disheartening, but yet

for nearly another hour, with the most unweary-
ing patience, both Herr Löhse and these servants
tried every device they could think of to get
them out, while other men lay in wait in the
background, ready, should either of them put
but a foot inside, to rush forward and push him
in ere he could retreat. All allurements, however, failed ; and at last, in despair, the cages
were removed and another experiment was
tried. The pails of milk were taken away to
the distant side of the enclosure, as far as
possible from the bath, and the men retreated
from sight, but not, however, from a point
of observation, from which they were within
easy reach of their victims. This device was
happily successful. Very soon, suspecting now
no danger, the unwieldy young pair waddled
out side by side and made for the enticing
draughts, and then they were captured. When
deep in their most innocent enjoyment, with
nose and eyes well buried in the pails, a strong
rope in the form of a noose was thrown swiftly
from behind, slipped rapidly over the astonished
heads, which were instantly raised, and drawn
securely but not painfully round the animals'
legs.

All was done in a moment, the dexterity

and cleverness of the Arabs in this performance being really marvellous. Powerless to kick or struggle, the captives were then lifted bodily into their boxes, the rope was removed, and the doors locked. Each box was then raised by means of long poles, fastened at the sides, extending both before and behind, to the shoulders of eight men, who carried them down the hill to the plain below, where the camels were waiting to receive them. They were then slung separately between two camels, who were harnessed in pairs side by side, at a sufficient distance apart from each other to admit of the boxes being placed between them, while a man walked at the head of each camel, leading it by a rope fastened firmly round its neck, with the additional small rope that goes through the nose also ready at hand to check any adverse movement that might threaten the safety of the precious burden!

The party set off by night, taking advantage of a moon which was nearly full; so these last preparations had not been commenced till the afternoon, and it was late in the evening before everything was ready for the first march, and our friends came to wish us good-bye.

Right sorry were we to feel that they were

really going, and we bid them most regretful
but hearty farewells, wishing them, it is needless
to say, every success and all prosperity in the
arduous and anxious undertaking that lay before
them.   They returned our greetings with kind-
est wishes for our well-being in our own novel
enterprise, but Herr Löhse repeated a warning,
which he had before many times urged, that I
should not remain in the country during the
remainder of the hot season.   He thought it
had already proved too trying, and that followed
by the rains, which are always more or less conducive to fever, the risk was very great.   Of
this we had ourselves already begun to entertain
serious doubts, but I was utterly unwilling, now
that we had come so far and gone through so
much, to give up our plans if by any possibility
they could be carried out, and the question had
remained as yet unsettled.

Before parting we drank "*bon voyage*" and
"*auf wiedersehen*" together, albeit in the "Lager
beer" which Germans love so well!—the three
gentlemen taking deep draughts, and I even
venturing to sip it for friendship's sake.   We
all "clinked glasses" together, conveying old-
world customs into this new world of the desert,
and bringing a dear sound of "home" to the

distant camp ; and then we watched them start. Most of the animals were already on the shore below, and some had even crossed the ford with their keepers ; the rest soon joined them, and as they all wended their way across the plain they looked a strange company, and one which could never have been seen except in such a land as we were then in. Our friends, bringing up the rear, stopped when they came to a corner, where a great cliff, that I shall soon tell you of, would take them from our sight, and turned round to wave a last adieu ; farewell shouts were exchanged, and then they were gone ! We turned back into the verandah feeling quite forlorn, and I cannot tell you how we missed that evening the sweet familiar concertina.

LETTER XXIII.

Beguiling the time—After the rains—A good growl—Ahmed
quite spoilt—I remonstrate with him—His impudence
seals his fate—I flatter myself that I triumph—Fear of
fire—Woke by a lion's roar—Dogs chained to my bedstead—Debûs guards the wicket—My early ride—The
lovely pool—My pet crocodile and hippo—Arabs water
their flocks—The daily struggle—The nights are cold.

EL GWAIYA, 10th *April.*

I MUST beguile the time by beginning a letter
to you to-day, even if I shall not be able to
finish it, for I am left now entirely to my own
society! I felt so much better at the beginning
of the week that I persuaded Charlie to start
on a shooting expedition, so he left for six days
and has gone to a place called Ombréga,
about ten miles off, which is to be his head-
quarters. We had endless consultations before
he started about our prospects and plans, for
this miserable illness of mine has disconcerted
us sadly, and we have really not known what
it would be best to do!

Our intention, on leaving Kassala, of going

to Jira, which we heard was full of game, and consequently excellent for shooting, Herr Löhse dissuaded us from, saying Jira was unhealthy, and he recommended instead a place called Collalāb, near Jira, which is said to be equally good for sport, but on higher ground, and consequently less likely to be affected by the malaria that is so prevalent in the lowlands after the rains. *That*, we are universally told, is the most dangerous time of the whole year, far more so than the rains themselves, or even than the hot weather. When the ground begins to get dry again, after it has been completely soaked, poisonous unwholesome vapours arise from the decaying vegetation and produce all kinds of sicknesses. Even the natives constantly suffer at that season, and to Europeans it is particularly injurious.

The best precautions are to be in the most elevated situation one can find, to have substantial dwelling-places built, and never to sleep in the open air. Nothing is more conducive to fever than that. It was with an especial view to this season that we intended to have the wooden houses put up, about which we consulted the Scotchman at Kassala.

To Collalāb, therefore, our thoughts have

turned, but whether after all we shall remain in
the country or not is yet a moot point; and
meanwhile I must tell you how I pass my days
when I am by myself. But before I begin I
must have a good *growl!* You cannot imagine
the untold world of trouble we have had with
the men and servants ever since we left Kassala;
they are even worse than those that were with
us before we reached it.

Read Sir Samuel Baker's *Nile Tributaries*,
for that will show you exactly the kind of annoy-
ances I speak of. While Charlie was here I
was only half aware of them, for he invariably
took all the trouble on himself, and I scarcely
knew of the difficulties; but now that I am alone
I have found out how intolerable in a hundred
ways these people really are. The camel men
are all of a different tribe from those that came
with us from Suakin, being Hamrans, not
Hadendoas, and many of our servants are
changed also. Ahmed and Hussein are still
with us, and also "Biri Biri," but the indiscriminate host of minor assistants are new; and
a dogged, obstinate race they are.

To call these hangers-on servants is almost
a farce, for they really have to be shown how
to do every single thing they are asked to put

their hands to; yet it is not their ignorance I complain of,—that, with a willing heart, can always be rectified,—it is their utter unreliability and laziness. If one did not superintend every single thing one's self, from sending them out for such daily supplies as are to be had in the neighbouring village, principally eggs and fowls, to feeding the dogs and sweeping out the compound and camel-sheds, nothing would be done, or, at any rate, only half done, and you know how miserable such a state of matters always is. The most disappointing thing has been to find that Ahmed, who seemed so invaluable before, has, since leaving Kassala, come out in quite a different light. His residence there has apparently spoiled him completely, dissipated his obliging nature and good qualities, and left him sulky, impertinent, and insufferable in a hundred ways.

This contrast between his former excellence and his present deficiencies is most striking, and I cannot yet get over my astonishment at the change in him. I sometimes feel inclined to think it must actually be his "double," if such a thing exists! and that it cannot be the bright pleasant fellow that used to serve us so willingly in every way, and whom we were so fond of. He has turned out to be a petty thief, a cheat, and utterly untruthful ; added to which he is indolent to the last degree, while he occasionally assumes an unbearable self-assertion which amounts to insolence.

In spite of the unpleasantness which has arisen from these faults, there has, after all, been something ineffably ludicrous now and then in my wordy tussles with him, and I have occasionally laughed to myself afterwards at the amusing recollections they afforded. Matters culminated one day when I found that it was undeniable that he had stolen at least half the morning portion of milk intended for Elfie and Fairy, this being the more aggravating as it could not be replaced, and these young dogs now refuse to take any other kind of food, yet it is absolutely necessary that they shall be well nourished or they will certainly die, for, having already suffered so much on the marches, they have become very delicate and require great care. I had him called up to the verandah, where I was sitting, and accused him at once of the theft, feeling that if I allowed it to pass on this occasion the repetitions would be unceasing, and I took the opportunity, too, to remonstrate more fully as to his general behaviour than I had done before.

The charge was of course instantly denied, and this was accompanied by an impudence which has sealed his fate. I can endure him no longer, and on Charlie's return shall certainly beg that he may be dismissed at once.

He slouched along to where I was sitting with an intolerably impertinent gait, and stood up before me, lolling against one of the posts of the verandah with an attitude of daring sauciness while I had my say. This was of course in broken Arabic, every syllable of which was nearly put to flight by my indignation at his posture and appearance, my words invariably failing at the very moments I most desired to bring them out with effect!

He waited till I had finished, having thoroughly understood, and known the truth too, of what I said, and then capped all his former delinquencies with a refinement of impertinence which was amusing as well as amazing. He gabbled off, as fast as he could utter it, a lot of Arabic, of which he was pretty well aware that I knew scarcely a single syllable, cleverly introducing, however, here and there a word which I had just used in speaking to him, and which consequently pointed to the accusations I had made, and made it appear as though I understood him. It instantly occurred to me to take his cue, and though I fear it may not have been very dignified, I could not resist it.

He understands a little English, and considering for a moment what words connected with his errors he was most familiar with, I assumed a sarcastic attitude, and responded in a rapid stream of my own language, of which he knew full well the drift, especially as I occasionally interspersed a little Arabic, assuring him in that language that he was a cheat, a thief, a liar, and *altogether* bad; and the sting of the reproof was, I trust, increased by his inability to follow me entirely. I then rose and swept grandly past him into the house, leaving him with every appearance of being crestfallen and disconcerted, for he had evidently understood that I had finally said he should be turned off, and I looked too much in earnest for him to doubt the threat.

11th April. I could not get further yesterday, I felt so tired and feverish, but I will go on again for a bit to-day.

The night succeeding my altercation with Ahmed I was terribly haunted by the dread that revenge might suggest itself to him in the form of fire. There had been an evil light in his handsome eyes which had not augured well, and for a long time I could not sleep, so possessed was I with this possible terror.

One tiny spark on these parched withering grass huts, and where should we be? with everything gone and without shelter under the blazing sun of an African desert. To save anything would be totally impossible, perhaps even in the general panic the camels might be lost, and our precious dollars, the only means we should have of getting fresh ones to take us back to civilised regions, would be gone too, reduced in five minutes to a lump of molten silver, afterwards only to be discovered in this shapeless form beneath the ruins. It would not be an irretrievable, but for a time an awkward, situation. Fire is, as I feared long ago it would be, my constant dread; and also, just as I foresaw, the innumerable rules I make about it are never regarded; indeed, I own myself that it would be extremely difficult to adhere to any rules that would prevent an accident; and the matter is, after all, simply one that must be left to chance and fate.

No small fire will burn in the open, as the intense heat of the sun would extinguish it, so by day the fires for cooking are always under a

straw shed, and it is a constant marvel to me .
that sparks do not ignite the roof; and at night
two large fires are always kept up in the centre
of the zareeba, some distance apart from each
other, to prevent wild beasts from prowling
round and disturbing us with their noise. Even
with this precaution hyenas often come up
quite close, though they cannot get in on
account of the thorny hedge. We see their
footmarks outside on the sand in the morning;
and last night I was startled from my sleep by
a terrific roar, which came, no doubt, from a
lion that was evidently taking a survey just
outside that very part of the thicket nearest to
which is my room.

It made me wince, I can assure you; although
I knew I was perfectly safe; and the poor dogs
that sleep at the foot of my bed started up and
trembled, and even when I spoke to them
reassuringly they still cowered, and it was long
before they would lie down again.   How amused
and perhaps amazed too you would be to see
me at night!   Now that I am by myself in the
huts, I always have these dear protectors near
me, and as they disturbed me at first a good
deal by running in and out, and barking in
reply to all the stray dogs that they heard in

the distance, the number of which is legion, I have since had Elfie and Fairy chained to my bedstead, and Debûs to the outer door. They appear to approve of the situation, and remain tolerably still, though low growls from one or other of them, and sometimes from all three, warn me occasionally that there are unwelcome strangers (either biped or quadruped) about, for whom they are ever on the alert; but no one, I am sure, would venture to approach while they are here. I always have my revolver, too, under my pillow, loaded and ready for an emergency, but *that* I trust will never occur.

There are two entrances to this well-guarded apartment of mine—one from the outer room, in which our baggage is stored, and which we also make the "dining-room"; and one from the zareeba itself at the opposite side. This latter entrance is merely a tall wicket gate fastened with a latch (there is not even a bolt), which might be easily unfastened by a hand stealthily passed between the bars; so it is at this entrance that faithful Debûs takes up his station, being, as I said, chained to it in case he should feel inclined to play truant; and I defy the boldest ruffian to pass him without suffering for it; should any one even endeavour to do so, he

would give me plenty of warning to bring my
revolver to the front and alarm the camp.   But
I have again wandered far from the description
of my day, of which I intended at the outset
to give you a sketch.

I rise about half-past five and rouse the
servants.   This is happily accomplished without
difficulty, as Sher Ullah, who sleeps in the
verandah, wakes very easily and gets up the
rest.   I then have a cup of tea or coffee and
munch some biscuits, after which I mount my
donkey, and, attended generally by Hussein and
another man, and accompanied by the dogs,
descend the path to the river-shore, cross the
Settit—which is now merely a narrow stream,
and in some places almost dry—and go out for
about a mile, over a rather uneven bit of ground,
till I get to a most lovely place near some great
black cliffs which rise up several hundred feet
high on either side.   Under the shadow of
these cliffs there is an immense pool which
never gets dry, and by it I dismount and sit
down in the shade on a lovely strip of smooth
sand to read and enjoy the scene.

This pool is about a hundred yards in length
by fifty broad, and the depth of the water is
from twelve to fifteen feet.   It is full of fish,

both large and small, which continually jump in and out, splashing delightfully and making a cool refreshing sound ; and it is also the home at present of a big crocodile and a hippopotamus. You cannot imagine how fond I am of both these huge creatures, and how I watch every morning for them. They are capital companions in my solitude. The crocodile sometimes becomes quite venturesome in the deep silence all round, now and then giving a tremendous leap and coming half out of the water, but occasionally he is much more cautious, and only ventures to put up the end of his long black nose quite timidly for a quiet sniff. Of the hippo, although I love him and like to know he is there, I have never seen more than the very extremity of his broad snout, for he seems to be extremely nervous, and has kept carefully underneath whenever we have been near the pool, so we came to the conclusion some time ago that he must have been already shot at, and has not yet forgotten the occurrence.

Charlie promised, when first we found them both out, never for my sake to molest them, so I now consider that they are my own special property. It is a fascinating spot, this little nook beneath the rocks, with a view up and down the river of about three hundred yards in all, and the sweet impression of it will remain with me all my life long. It is perfectly secluded, and combines a calm peacefulness and a wild romance that give it a peculiar charm; it is just the sort of place, in fact, in which to lie for ever, dreaming on the "yellow sand"! Wild fowl, with lazily flapping wings, cross the water now and then with a half-discordant cry, well suited to the loneliness of the scene, and Arabs come down from the opposite hills, bringing their flocks and herds to drink. They rest under a large feathery tree upon the brink of the river, and call ever and anon to their cattle in strange but melodious tones, that chime in well with the place and time.

About eight o'clock I regretfully remember that the sun has already become too hot for me to remain out any longer, so I beckon to the men, who have gone far away to smoke their hookahs, to bring "Prince" back, and call to the dogs, which, after rushing wildly about in the cool freshness all over the sand, have at last lain down beside me, and are now fast asleep; and then I mount my donkey, and we all go briskly home.

The next scene presents probably a "striking contrast." An hour's struggle with the domestics is certain to ensue. Directions are given for the day, and complaints heard and made! Things done that should not have been done, are ordered if possible to be undone, and those that are left undone are ordered to be done! and there are always abundance of *both* ready at hand you may be quite sure. Both my Arabic and my temper are always sorely tried during this hour; the latter, I own, generally suffering the more severely of the two!

About half-past nine I go into my room, put on cool things, take some slight refreshment, read, write letters, learn Arabic, do needlework (calculate daily the probable time to Charlie's return!), and have perhaps, if I am very tired, or more than usually feverish, a short nap, though that does not often occur so early in the day. All this time the tiresome intermittent fever still lasts, and in spite of my getting up and going about I am not unfrequently obliged to take the "thirteen grains" of quinine at night that Dr. Bijorath ordered me when it was much worse, for I have a dread of its returning in full force.

About one o'clock I have my lunch-break-
fast, after which comes a proper siesta, and
about 4.30 it is needless, I am sure, for me to
tell you *what* I have, for you know quite well
already.   Only now my tea is not made in the
" kettle," but in a certain little China teapot that
went with me, I won't say how many years
ago, to India, and is now here in Africa, having
accompanied me, in fact, wherever I have
travelled.   After that, when the sun is nearing
the horizon, I either go and sit in the verandah, which has then become cool enough, or
down to the shore again for an hour or two.

At half-past seven I dine, and go to bed
soon after nine! and I assure you, though I am
by myself, and often wish for a companion
(provided the companion were congenial!), the
day never seems wearisome.

I have not yet told you how surprisingly cold
the nights are.   This is an inexpressible bless-
ing, though to me a most incomprehensible fact.
The thermometer goes down to 50° and lower,
and I sleep under four or five woollen coverings,
one of them an English blanket, deliciously soft
and thick ; and the water taken from the skins
in the morning is even more liked iced water
than it used to be six weeks ago.

LETTER XXIV.

EL GWAIYA, 13*th April.*

I HAD the delight yesterday of receiving another
packet of home letters, the second now since
leaving Suez. They were brought by Abdullah—one of the soldiers lent us by the Pasha—
who had gone into Kassala a few days before
to take our own letters to the post office, to ask
for others, and to get fresh stores.

One letter was from you, dearest mother, of
course ; I always know that, whoever else does
or does not write, I can count upon *your* having
done so, and this is a real kindness for which I
can never sufficiently thank you. In this far-off
land, after weeks of waiting, to feel that when
the mail comes in it will be sure to bring a long

home-budget, telling one about everything and everybody, is a never-failing source of happy anticipation, and carries one happily through a hundred *longing* moments. Letters at this distance, and with the extreme uncertainty as to their time of arrival, have altogether a different meaning to one from those that can come at any time by the regular three or four daily posts of even every little provincial town at home ; and in London, where one is almost surfeited with the superabundance of deliveries, it seems to me one knows nothing of the real happiness of receiving a letter.

Just now, in Charlie's absence, this mail has been particularly acceptable. I had nine delicious long letters, some very amusing. It is a feast over which I shall be happy for a long time. The soldier who brought them is such a trustworthy good man, quite unlike the other who stole the water and whom we have never liked, and, in addition to his many merits, he luckily speaks French very well, having been in Cairo a great deal and picked it up there. He has plenty of intelligence ; though, oddly enough, he looks rather a thick stupid old fellow, but he takes in everything at a glance, and is a great comfort to me.

His comrade, like Ahmed, has caused me annoyance lately in a variety of ways; so I took Abdullah down with me to the shore, when I went for my evening walk, and poured out all my grievances to him; and now, having put him up to things, I feel sure that all will go straighter. The other servants are profoundly jealous of my talking to him in a language which they cannot understand, but I am so desperately angry with them that I feel inclined to do it all the more! and, though I fear it is rather deficient in dignity, I occasionally take an opportunity of calling Abdullah up and holding forth, in either a confidential manner—which I can see nearly drives them mad—or an emphatic one, with occasional slight gestures in the direction of the kitchen, that are, I own, calculated to raise all their ire, as they probably think (and rightly) that I am telling him of their own wrong-doings.

I have misgivings that this may end in Abdullah being quite spoiled, and the rest growing more alienated than they were before; but their conduct all this time, when they ought to have taken extra care of me, has been so exasperating that I cannot resist the temptation of having a little revenge now! To avert the

likelihood of spoiling Abdullah I play off Sher
Ullah against him by talking confidentially
about lamps or the cleaning of my boots in
Malay, when he is, of course, quite as much at
sea as the others are when I speak French.
Sher Ullah himself really deserves a medal.   I
don't know how I should have got on without
him.   He and all his ways are as clean as a
pin, and he works all day splendidly.   He is
my own especial servant, and looks after all
table matters, keeps my room also as tidy as it
could be kept, polishes up my boots as though
I were going to walk down Rotten Row in
them, trims the lamps to perfection, and does a
thousand other little things just as well as when
we were in the Malay Straits.   He cannot do
everything, however, and so, in many ways, I
am obliged to be dependent upon the others
too ; Ahmed, for instance, always cooks.   The
dislike which Sher Ullah had from the first to
these Arabs does not at all diminish, and, indeed,
he may be now said to hate them.   The lofty
contempt which arose in his soul when he saw
them " eating the eyes " at Lagua has considerably increased, but though troubles sometimes
arise from his not pulling well with them, yet he
keeps so much by himself that this is not a

serious evil.   Difficulties most frequently occur from his not understanding their language, for he will not attempt to acquire it, and even now only knows a few words.

He is madly enthusiastic to learn English, and my morning occupations are varied by teaching him to read and write.   He has picked up an immense deal already, though, curiously enough, he scarcely began to learn it till he came to Africa ; and, as he has a capital memory, is getting on well.   We began by telling him the names of familiar objects in daily use, and then short sentences were added ; but apparently he has not a very fine ear, for similar sounds confuse him terribly.   He cannot yet discern the difference between " paper " and " pepper," or between " sheep " and " ship," and he occa-sionally makes a most amusing jumble by using adjectives that are wholly inappropriate to the nouns in question.   For instance, he would insist on assuring me this morning that the cat was *red!* and after denying this fact and suggesting every colour I could possibly think of as appropriate, each one of which seemed to confuse him more than the last, it suddenly struck me that he meant " dead," which I found was the fact !

The other day he was equally persistent
that the moon was *bull*, by which I suppose he
wished to intimate that it was *full*.   However, on the whole, he deserves great credit
for the progress he has made, especially considering that, except by myself at the time of
his lessons, he never hears English spoken, and
I have reason, I think, to be proud of my pupil!

I have been suffering very much during the
last two days from the "simoom"; the scorching, suffocating nature of this wind is not to be
described.   It has penetrated even into the
house, thick and well built as it is, and the
whole atmosphere has been full of a yellowish
red colour, which is simply produced by minute
particles of sand that completely fill it when
this wind is blowing, and which are wafted into
everything.   This is the wind that sometimes
brings up the destructive fatal sandstorms in
which people are lost.   It is an extraordinary
thing that, in spite of this simoom, the thermometer is unaccountably low.   I can scarcely
believe, although I see it, that it stands at only
78°, the pleasant temperature of Penang hill, yet
here the heat is simply unendurable.   I have
often much wished, since being in this country,
that I knew something about atmospheric in-

fluences, so as to be able to account in some measure for the strange occurrences that take place ; this lowness of the thermometer, for instance, the cold nights, the gales that so often blow here, etc. etc., but alas ! I fear I have neglected that part of my education.

15*th*. Charlie returned yesterday evening, a day sooner than I expected him. He came earlier "to give me a pleasant surprise," he said ; and in reply I told him that "vanity was the chief weakness of all men"! He had shot two hippos, a crocodile, a "tetal," a kudu, and several antelopes ; and he had also had a shot at a lion, but as that was by moonlight, and at a distance of three hundred yards, it is not surprising that the enemy escaped.

He was, however, disappointed at not getting elephants. For that sport, at this season of the year, it is evident that to be well mounted is indispensable. The elephants during the hot weather remain the whole day long in the thickest parts of the jungle, and only come out on to the open, or down to the rivers to drink, at night, when, in the uncertain light, shooting them would be attended with much risk, and to follow them to the distant forests to which they return before the sun has risen—twenty miles or more inland—and to pursue them, if when once roused or wounded they ran, it would be absolutely necessary to have strong swift horses.

These could be procured, and we should get them if we were going to remain in the plains, as we at first intended to do ; but since Charlie has been away he has universally heard such bad accounts of the unhealthiness of the lowlands from June to October that, after another long talk and consultation, we have decided not to risk remaining in them.

The necessity for going has been a great disappointment to us both, as the natives tell us that the shooting on the Settit is very good, and easily obtained during the rains. Contrary to their custom in the hot weather, elephants at that time of year come down in the daytime to the rivers,—which are then swollen to rapid torrents, the water being not only level with the banks but often overflowing them,—and after satisfying their thirst they retire to the neighbouring little valleys, which are then covered with grass, and where also the trees and bushes are in full leaf, so that in these pleasant retreats they find both food and shade, and in them, poor things, are easily tracked and shot!

I ought to have told you long ago what you

are not perhaps aware of, and what indeed I
did not realise myself till lately, that this is
Charlie's first hot season in the plains of Africa.
I am sure this will astonish you as it did me,
for I fancied he knew the country in every phase
and aspect. He was in this part of it fifteen
years ago, but left it, as hunters always do, at
the end of March, and his long periods in Africa
have been always in Abyssinia. While there
he invariably spent the hot season in the hills,
so that it is as new to him as it is to me to
find himself in the scorching plains of an African
desert. This has consequently been an experi-
mental trip for both of us, and we have had,
and still have, to find out much as to climate,
localities, etc. etc.

All this I like immensely, but it is quite
possible that, from our newness to everything,
our plans may often change, and they are even as
yet too much in embryo for me to speak of anything with certainty. As we are to leave the
plains we have determined to go to a country
called Bogos, on the north-west border of
Abyssinia—which is perfectly healthy, being
very mountainous, and consequently free from
malaria — and we have already commenced
preparations for the journey. We are told that

there is a little community of Europeans already
settled there in one of the towns called Keren.
I think they are principally the members of a
Catholic mission, but it will be nice to feel that
we have neighbours of our own race not far
off; and they will doubtless be able to put us
up to many a wrinkle regarding our future,
as they have been established in the land some
years.

To reach Bogos we shall have to return to
Kassala to get fresh camels, as our Hamran
drivers and all their tribe are at enmity with
the tribes near Abyssinia, and they consequently
will not take us in that direction. Feuds are
not unfrequent between the various tribes in
the Soudan, who occasionally make raids into
each other's dominions, carrying off cattle and
destroying each other's crops; and we do
not wish to fall victims to an existing state of
illwill with which we have nothing whatever
to do.

We find that there is a route from this
eastern side of the Soudan by which we can
escape a portion at least of that part of the
desert which has no water; and as we shall
take double the supply with us that we had last
time, and make the journey more leisurely, I

think there is no probability of our suffering as we did before.

But I must not forget, while we are still here, to tell you about the hippos that Charlie shot at Ombréga. How he got them would scarcely interest you; but I want, if I can, to convert you to the idea of hippopotamus *soup*, for you really cannot imagine how good it is; and if you will not think that I have become altogether barbarous, I will describe the preparations. After the animal has been shot (I will begin with that preliminary!), the flesh is cut off and at once "jerked,"—that is, sliced up into long strips which are spread out in the sun to dry, and, when that process has been completed, piled together and tied up in bundles. A large camel-load of this meat was brought in yesterday from the two hippos, and is now stacked. It has been placed (how horrible you will think this) in a shed close by the verandah! This has been done (oh, worse and worse!) by my especial desire, in order that we may be able to keep in some measure an "eye upon it"; for, being the very favourite food of these good folk, it would most certainly be all gone in no time if they had not a wholesome dread of our proximity. Of the proximity of this curious

store we are not, astonished as you may be to
hear it, in the least aware through our olfactory
nerves—it has been too thoroughly dried for
that ; and, indeed, we make visits of inspection
now and again to see that it is not diminishing
faster than can be reasonably accounted for.
A goodly share having been bestowed upon the
domestics to begin with, we earnestly trust that
they will kindly allow us to retain our own, but
all the same it is a dangerously tempting dainty.
To make it into soup a strip is taken, and as
much as is deemed sufficient for the quantity
required is chopped up into smaller bits—for
the whole thing is as hard as a bone—and then
it is slowly boiled for hours.   It is extremely
nourishing, and more like good mock-turtle
soup than anything I can compare it to, though
I assure you that of the two I infinitely prefer
it, uncivilised as this taste may sound.   With a
few herbs added, and a little seasoning, it is
delicious, and the first thing I have really cared
for since my illness began.

We had a great disappointment about the
kudu.   When the baggage camels arrived
and we inquired for the horns—which, Charlie
told me, were unusually long, quite perfect, and
beautifully spiral—they were nowhere to be

found ; and it then came out that they had
been completely forgotten by these wretched
men, who, caring only for the meat, which in any
case they would have had, had left them behind.
They had cleverly skinned the animal (do not
shudder, remember that it was dead) from its
hind legs to its head, turning it in fact inside
out, and, having cut out all the best portions of
the meat, had put them into the bag thus made
and brought it away. This is the invariable
way in which the Arabs take home the meat of
any large animal.

20th April. Here we are within two days
of Kassala again, encamped for twenty-four
hours in our tent under a big tree, in order to
have a rest after the long march from the south.
We have managed it splendidly this time, having travelled always by night, taking advantage
of a glorious moon, and halting by day until it
was cool enough to go on again. My fever
has quite left me, and I am all the better for
the move.

We left El Gwaiya on the 16th, at 7 P.M.,
and made the first three marches through
districts where there were wells and villages, so
that considerably decreased the trying part ; and
now we have arrived again at wells, so there

have been no difficulties this time to speak of. Charlie insisted on having a sort of covered chair, called a *takhtawan*, made for me to commence the journey with, thinking I should not be able to bear the fatigue of riding, and men were sent out at early dawn the day before we started to cut poles for this *sedan*. With the most untiring ardour Abdullah and his master worked nearly all day long concocting and carrying out this great idea, and when it was completed there was without doubt enough of it to account for many hours of labour! The canopy was so vast that I was almost lost in it! As, however, more men than could be spared would assuredly have been required to carry it, with the addition of myself inside, this unrivalled throne was hoisted on to the back of a camel, from which elevation it arose like a beacon in the desert, and at this giddy height I took up my position.

Ingratitude is base, and I grieve to think that for a moment I should have seemed guilty of it; but the manner in which that marvellous erection rolled and shook, rendered it perfectly unendurable for more than half an hour. It was secure but not steady, and feeling terribly guilty I was obliged to abandon it and betake myself once more to dear " Wad Zaid," whose gentle paces carried me far more easily than even Indian *doolie* men could have done ; and when we reached our first halt after four hours' march, I was, thanks to him, none the worse and quite a marvel to myself.

We shall move on again to - morrow to Kassala, and there make all preparations for going to Bogos as quickly as we can, so as to reach it, if possible, in about a month from the present time, for after that the heat would be absolutely intolerable for travelling. It is baking enough now ! and even the nights are becoming hot, or it may be that they are always so at this season away from the rivers. The way in which our boxes are warped is marvellous to behold. It is fatal to open them on a march, as nothing will induce them to shut properly again until after they have been for some days in the shade ; and even then only by dint of such bangs, kicks, and pushes, as threaten to send the whole case to destruction, can the shrunken covers " be brought to." We try to remember all the things that will be required on the road before we start, and these are put into bags to prevent the necessity of opening the boxes, and whatever has been forgotten has to be done without; but that condition of things is one we are quite accustomed to now!

The dogs, by means of unceasing care, have not suffered as they did before in their backs, but if they run out of the tents in the daytime they cry with pain as they go over the hot ground; and I assure you I am not exaggerating in the very faintest degree when I tell you that the heat burns through my boots and is almost unendurable. I am rejoiced to think that we are to get away to a cool country, and only wish we could be off at once for it.

LETTER XXV.

"WITHIN A MILE" OF KASSALA
(NOT " EDINBURGH") TOWN !   28*th April*.

WE have pitched our tents in a large melon
garden about a mile from the town, preferring
to get all the breezes that may blow, scorching
as they are, to going into the stifling breathless
atmosphere of crowded Kassala. A huge mountain, over three thousand feet high, one bare
block of granite, rises up about a quarter of a
mile to our right, at the foot of which is a straggling bit of jungle, and between that and us
comes the high road, and then the garden in
which we are encamped.   It is very much the
same as the garden nearer Kassala which I
described before, only, alas ! it has not nearly so
many trees ; but we could not get the space there

that we have here, and in spite of this draw-
back were obliged to make the best of it.

Our old acquaintance, *Madame*, came, with
her little girl and a retinue of domestics, in the
most warm-hearted manner to give us a friendly
welcome directly she heard we had arrived, and
we had a long talk over all that had mutually
transpired in our histories since last we met.

Nothing eventful appears to be going on in
the town now. I evidently came in for "the
season" before, and scarcely think I shall pay
it many visits this time, especially as the heat
has increased so frightfully, but I must go in
one evening to call on the Pasha's wife and her
beautiful baby again! Bim Bashi, too, has
ridden over on his splendid charger, looking as
handsome as ever, and, having now made a little
progress with my Arabic, I was able to converse
more easily than before, which was a great
satisfaction!

One thing has happened that we are very
sorry for. Abdullah, the nice soldier, was re-
called yesterday to his duties. He was a right
good man to the end, above all spoiling, and we
parted from him with sincere regret. The other
man we had returned "with thanks" to the
Pasha (though with none to himself) immedi-

ately we arrived, but had retained Abdullah. However, as we have now had his services for so long, and are at present close to a town again, we felt that we could not possibly screw out any further excuse for keeping him, and he had to go.

A large detachment of soldiers was told off for duty to-day at a distant station, and, as they passed our camp, Abdullah, who was among them, left the ranks and ran over to speak to us for a minute. We were heartily glad to see him, but he said, alas! that there was no chance of his being allowed to come back to us.

An unmistakable proof of the advance of the season is the difference of temperature at night now. We are almost invariably obliged to sleep out-of-doors, and the tent is opened as wide as possible, directly the sun goes down, to cool it as completely as may be by the next morning ; but the chief thing that annoys me is the high wind, which now, strangely enough, so often blows at night. Refreshing it is, doubtless, to the whole land, but individually disturbing. One's breath is almost taken away sometimes, at unexpected moments, by a gale which sweeps ruthlessly over one, and makes sad havoc with the coverings, and we have had occasionally, at midnight, to get up and transport our bedsteads to the tent again for shelter.

Once there was such a terrific hurricane that, in spite of securing the tent in every way we could devise, it really seemed to me that each moment it would be carried away, and this fate really happened to poor Sher Ullah, who was sleeping in a very small tent not far off. The whole thing suddenly collapsed and came down upon him with a flop, and then the wind being extremely strong, and the tent and Sher Ullah both very light, they were rolled along together for a few yards, and I believe the poor boy ran imminent risk of being smothered in the canvas if Charlie had not become aware of the situation and rushed to the rescue!

Who do you think came to breakfast with us a few mornings ago? I am sure you will guess at once. Herr Löhse and Dr. Bijorath! We were delighted to find they had not left Kassala, but they were off that same day, and that was their farewell visit. They got over the march from the Settit without any catastrophe; the hippos are still alive and flourishing, and the elephants have behaved admirably. It is sincerely to be hoped that they will all get up as well to Suakin as they have so far. The number of animals being now increased by those that were already in the depôt here (making considerably over a hundred altogether), sixty camels are required solely for water on the march, and more than double the former number of goats for milk, and the magnitude of the undertaking is vastly increased.

4th May. You will be surprised to see that we are still here, but the fact is our plans have received a most cruel and disappointing blow. Everything was actually ready for our start. After infinite trouble and great delay we had hired the camels (even, according to the usual custom, advanced the drivers half their pay), bought supplies of durra and all manner of stores, engaged fresh servants, and even packed our boxes, when Charlie was told the very morning before we intended to be off that the Pasha could not permit us to go to Bogos. He at first thought this was a joke, and was treating it as one, when the officer delegated to spread this unpleasant dish before him quietly asserted that it was no joke but a fact.

Charlie, still half incredulous, but very indignant, then inquired the meaning of this prohibition, and also who could forbid him from going where he liked. The circumstances alleged are:

these : They say that there is, on the borders of Abyssinia, a rebel chief named Welda Inchael, who has deserted his country and come over to Egypt. This man has actually obliged Egypt to acknowledge him as an ally, but he has now grown beyond all power of control, and become simply a lawless freebooter. The Egyptian Government does not care to involve itself in the outlay and trouble of putting him down and he is therefore winked at. They say that they could not, for their own sakes, allow Europeans to fall into the hands of this rebel, and consequently that we must not go near him.

Filled with dismay as we are at these tidings we are yet more indignant that they were not made known to us before. Why have we been allowed to involve ourselves in all the loss of time and trouble, and in the outlay, too, to which we have gone, while the existence of this chief has been kept dark until the last moment ? The Pasha well knew the very first day we returned to Kassala, when Charlie saw his chief officer, and not only declared his intention of going to Bogos but asked advice about the whole plan, what our wishes were ; and we are filled with wrath that this hindrance, which has existed for months past, was not told us at once.

It is another proof of the selfish want of consideration of these phlegmatic people.

For a time after receiving this prohibition,
which we felt it would be utterly useless to
attempt to defy, as the Pasha could easily have
prevented our getting camels, we were completely at a loss, and knew not in the least what
to resort to. For a little bit we seriously contemplated returning to England until after the
rains, and then coming back again to Africa in
November; but this prospect was so unsatis-
factory that we soon gave it up. The mountains
near Suakin had been suggested by the Pasha's
emissary as a good hill place during the rains,
but this was not to be thought of for a moment.
To travel all the way back that we had already
come, taking that long wearisome journey that
had only just brought us to the part of the
country we wished to be in so soon again, would
have been too disheartening, and we would not
listen to the proposition. Besides, there would
be nothing to do at Suakin, no shooting, and
absolutely no interest of any kind for four or
five dreary months. No, such a prospect was
not to be even contemplated, so, after getting
further advice and weighing all circumstances,
we decided to run the risk of going to Collalāb

after all.   Meantime, however, we intend having a fortnight's shooting on the river Gāsh,
and are now making fresh preparations for the
journey there.

We have commissioned a Mohammedan
priest who lives at Collalāb, and who seems to
be quite the " Father of the village," to build us
some houses.   We drew out the plans with him
this morning and arranged the whole thing.
It was not a very difficult architectural business,
seeing that the mansion will comprise but two
rooms and a bath-room !   At a convenient distance will be the servants' houses ; every house
consisting merely of one small room, but were
there a sufficient number to give every man
one to himself, three or four of them would
be sure to congregate in each house from
choice.

The kitchen, and the various sheds for dogs,
donkeys, and camels, will complete the establishment.   They will all be made of grass, and the
whole will be surrounded by a stout zareeba.
This will, in fact, be our own special zareeba,
and you will be able, I am sure, to picture it to
yourself.   The expense of these winter or rainy
quarters is the most amusing part of the whole
affair.   They will not cost us above six or seven

pounds at the outside, and that will allow for all sorts of little extra luxuries that the residences of the natives do not usually contain.

The stout poles that are required for the roof and framework of these houses is the chief

FAKI ALI.

part of the cost; men often have to be sent some distance to get these, and it is not always easy to find the right kind of grass—long and wiry—to make the superstructure of. At this season especially, when everything is already so very much burned up, a little additional outlay will very likely have to occur before it is procured. The name of the priest who is going to undertake all this for us is Faki Ali, and as he is quite a *character* I must describe him.

His most obvious virtue is that he is spotlessly clean, and I only wish that many a continental priest could take a lesson from him. Of burly proportions and jovial mien, he is not in countenance at all unlike a merry friar, but the snowy whiteness of his ample robes would contrast with infinite advantage by the side of their sombre garments, and sometimes not overbathed appearance. I have a suspicion, nevertheless, that, like many of his brethren of whatever creed, he is not deficient in an eye to the main chance ; and that a good deal, perhaps, of the devoted politeness we have received from him is bestowed with a view to obtaining a request which he has pertinaciously proffered for the last few days. This is for the loan of a hundred dollars to buy ivory with, he says. The percentage he purposes to make by this outlay is, however, of such fabulous proportions that we rather doubt his actual design in the matter. It has been necessary to entrust him with a small sum of money on our own account as a preliminary for the commencement of our houses ; but in spite of his robes of whiteness I had uncomplimentary misgivings, as they were put into his hands, as to whether they would ever be applied to the purpose they were intended for.

One service he has done us, however, which has been very acceptable,—he has made us a lot of "*tej*." This is the beer of the country, and I think when well made that it is a most fascinating drink. It is composed principally of honey, with a small quantity of the bark of a particular tree ground to powder, which is put in to ferment it ; another ingredient is added to flavour it, and the mixture is then poured into stone jars, corked tightly down, and buried in the ground to keep it cool, for the process of fermentation is so rapid that tej can only be used when one is remaining in one place for any length of time ; were it to be taken on a march in the hot sun the bottles would assuredly burst.

8th May. There really seems to be some prospect of our getting off at last to-morrow, though a most singular hitch has arisen this time in the way of our getting camels. The owners have been afraid to bring them into Kassala from the outlying districts, as a Government order has just been issued to procure a certain number and send them out into the distant forests to bring in timber for repairing the telegraph poles throughout the Soudan. This is always a golden opportunity for the oppression and extortion exercised by the common soldiers. Twice the number of camels that are required are invariably seized in the name of the Government, and never relinquished until such tribute is paid by the owners as the soldiers choose to demand, which "tribute" they of course appropriate for themselves.

We have, however, been finally able to procure a sufficient number for our baggage, and trust that nothing will now prevent our going. The heat of this Kassala plain has become intolerable; even my *cyeballs* have seemed terribly scorched of late, and no relief is to be obtained from fanning one's self, as the air, when put in motion, resembles that which comes from a furnace. I am quite sick of our melon garden, romantic as it sounds, and will gladly change it for another locality.

Our priestly adviser paid us a farewell visit last evening, and I must tell you of a conversation I had with him, which showed me, even more clearly than I was before aware of, how women in the East are absolutely without choice in the matter of their marriages, these affairs being evidently arranged for them by the will or convenience of others without the slightest reference to their own wishes. I was taking a turn by myself in the garden, Charlie having gone into Kassala on business, when the visitor arrived. Making "a virtue of necessity," I utilised the occasion by diligently exercising my Arabic. We discussed a variety of subjects, and finally fell upon marriage-customs in England. Faki Ali was most interested in this topic, and extremely anxious to hear all about it, so I described everything; but when it came to courtship, and the possibility of the lady saying "no," he turned upon me with a polite smile, beneath which, however, I clearly saw that he simply believed me to be romancing.

I reiterated my assertions and enlarged upon the theme, even descanting on the occasional shyness and timidity of the wooer in my country, and intimated that before marriage at any rate the lady had it all her own way! His amazement was boundless, but I was certain the whole time that he scarcely believed a word I said. This suspicion was confirmed on Charlie's return by his adroitly introducing our late conversation, and repeating in incredulous tones the marvellous things that I had been relating.

He was, poor man, not a little dismayed to find that they were confirmed, having evidently hoped that the half of them at least would be explained away ; but I still have a suspicion that he thought even then that my assertions were supported merely out of loyalty, and that such a dangerous condition of "free will" in womankind was beyond the limits of all possible belief.

Having, nevertheless, survived this shock to his feelings he returned with redoubled wariness to the petition which was without doubt the sole cause of his visit, and I am mean enough to say that I regret to state he gained his point. His importunity, which absolutely amounted to a gentle kind of dogged bullying, won him the day. It was certainly rather a consideration that if he had not got this (which, I am bound to say, he declares no power shall prevent him from returning) he would have probably appropriated that which had been given him to use for us, and when the rains commence, and we arrive at Collalāb for shelter, we might find not a vestige of a hut, but instead only plausible excuses.

After obtaining what he wished, he graciously consented to remain and dine with us.   It is a puzzle to me how he reconciled our dishes to his conscience but so he did, and played a capital knife and fork too! I ought not to say knife and fork though, for after struggling quite ineffectually with these weapons for a few minutes (the first time in his life probably that he had ever wielded them) he relinquished the effort with a heavy sigh, and with an elaborate bow and laboured apology requested to be permitted to return to his accustomed habit of eating with his fingers.

Having in this manner reduced a good-sized fowl to a skeleton, he washed his hands by having water poured over them Arab fashion, and I regretted that we had nothing but Kassala soap to offer him, which, as to its cleansing power, has very little effect, I fear. I grieve to say that our own supply of European soaps is finished; would that we had brought double or treble the quantity, for we have now to fall back upon this country stuff, and most abominable it is. The two only ingredients in it, I am firmly persuaded, are lime and grease, the lime pre-ponderating. It is so excessively hard that it is almost impossible to get anything off, rub as one will, and what does come makes one's hands as rough as a nutmeg-grater. The manufacturer of this poor stuff I cannot but compassionate, inclined to quarrel with him as I am, for he is one of the victims of the Government dishonesty. They owe him hundreds of dollars, for he has made soap for the garrison for years past, and is now an elderly man ; but he can get neither his money nor redress.

It is a most heartless and unfair state of things, and fills me with indignation. He is a Greek, and longing to go back to his country to spend his remaining years among his own people, but he is positively not allowed to go. Unless, too, he could take with him the result of his lifelong toil he would scarcely wish to return, for he would find himself penniless after all these years, and perhaps be obliged at his advanced age to begin life again. Truly in a thousand ways the Soudan and all its inhabitants are groaning under the yoke of Egypt, as the Israelites of old groaned under it during the time of their captivity.

LETTER XXVI.

HAIKOTA, 13*th May.*

ONCE again we are encamped in the neighbourhood of a river, though that, after all, does not
really express the situation, for we are actually
in the dry bed of one—that of the river Gāsh
or Māreba, which runs south-east of Kassala.
We have come down to this place merely for
a fortnight's shooting; and, as we were to be
absent for only a short time, we stored almost
all our baggage in the warehouse of the friendly
German merchant at Kassala, and came in light
marching order.

We shall return to Kassala when our trip
here is over, pick up what we have left there,

and go to Collalāb on the Settit for the rains,
hoping to reach it by the 1st of June. The
minimum of luggage for this fortnight is represented by nine camel-loads, we could not get
it into a smaller compass, do what we would—
but this is considerably less than half our usual
quantity.

The Indian tent, which we never like to be
without, is one camel-load in itself; and we had
to bring a larger supply than usual of durra for
both animals and servants, as, at this season, it
will probably be difficult to procure in out-of-
the-way places; while rifles, ammunition, cooking apparatus, angrébs, rolls of bedding, two
boxes of clothes, and one camel-load of water,
complete the tale. In coming to Haikota on
the Gāsh, though again going south of Kassala,
we were on a much more easterly direction
than before when we went to the Settit, and
this time we did not pass through a country
without water.

We had intended to march in the dry bed of
the river, as smoother and less fatiguing for the
camels than over the uneven stony plains; but,
to our surprise, on reaching it we found that it
was flooded for a considerable distance by rain,
which had fallen unexpectedly in the high lands

the previous night, so we were obliged to cross, and keep along the bank on the left-hand side.

It was a most difficult business for the camels to get over, for, though we were able to find a tolerably good ford, yet the whole ground was wet and slimy, and they slipped terribly, and were dreadfully nervous. Camels have a horror of damp ground, as you know, I am sure ; their smooth flat feet can find no foothold, and their fear increases the probability of their falling ; when that happens, the result is indeed grievous—their legs slide away from under them, going in contrary directions, and I have been told that they actually split up, and become perfect wrecks !

Nothing so terrible as this, however, occurred to us now, but we had to go very cautiously, and it took a long time. The delay of our getting fairly off upon the march was increased, too, by Sher Ullah discovering, just as we were about to cross the river, that he had dropped or left behind him the keys of all the boxes under his charge, containing stores, wines, table appointments, lamps, and cooking apparatus, etc. etc. These keys had—since the first loss when the gold chain was stolen—been long ago replaced at Kassala, and as we really could

not again go through the inconvenience we
had already suffered, we halted, while several
of the men, and Sher Ullah himself, went back
quite half a mile to look for them. After an
hour's delay they returned in triumph, having
found them on the ground close by where the
boxes had been packed, and we then set off in
earnest.

About midnight we came to within a quarter
of a mile of a very large Arab village called
Shariff. It was only eight miles from Kassala,
though, owing to the delays, we had been five
hours in reaching it; and here, to our dismay
and consternation, the guide—who had professed,
as they all do, to know the way perfectly—now
owned to being unable to find it in the dark;
and, as the moon would set in an hour, he said
we must halt. This was most aggravating, as
we then saw that we should have to travel by
day, and we knew what killing work that would
now be; however, there was no help for it, so,
resolving to be off as early as possible in the
morning, the old story was repeated over again.
No tent was pitched, but our angrébs were put
down at one side of the camp, and we slept in
the open.

The drivers had a great dread of thieves

from this village,—giving the people a very bad character ; so they kept watch all night by a big fire, drew up the camels, as on former marches, round it, and piled the baggage in a heap close by. I was at first utterly at a loss how to make my toilette, for there was nothing whatever on the plain in the way of a screen, —not a bush, nor even one of the big ant-hills, that might have served this purpose,—and the moon made everything as light as day, while the watchfire also was burning brightly. The difficulty seemed rather appalling, when I luckily bethought me of a big umbrella,—got on to my bedstead, fixed the umbrella up to the side, and under this friendly shelter was as snug as possible.

Before daylight next morning I awoke and dressed, while it was still too dark to be seen. Then came a privation which I had not anticipated,—for the first time in our journeyings there was not enough water for me to wash my face! We had come in as light marching order as possible, bringing only one camel-load of water-skins, and, as there now appeared to be great uncertainty as to the distance to the next village, every drop had to be saved for drinking.

We started as soon as ever it was light enough to see the way, and went on till eleven o'clock, when we reached the next halting-ground, a lovely place close by the river-side, called the Wells of Newaima. But oh, what trouble we had had to find the way! This guide was the greatest deceiver of any into whose hands we had yet fallen, and the track appeared to be as new to him as it was to us.

Every Arab we met or passed, we tried to press into our service to show us the road, and at last, after constantly going astray, we were put upon the right track by an old fellow whom we had known before at El Gwaiya, one Haji Musa, who was himself wandering about in search of two of his camels that seemed to be hopelessly lost. At the wells, however, we were amply compensated for all the previous worries. It was one of those exceptional spots that will for ever stand out in my memory as a true oasis in the desert.

Quite unlike either Wandik, Aradeb, or the pool at El Gwaiya, it was nevertheless exceedingly charming. A large clearing had been made in the midst of a dense jungle, while magnificent trees towered overhead, on which there was much more leaf than we had seen for a long time. The neighbouring inhabitants told us that here there was always more water than at any other place along the Gāsh during the dry weather. Had there been no leaves the magnificent network of lacy branches that spread in every direction would have been pretty enough as the sunlight came glinting through them, making delicious lights and shadows; though, even with so much shade around, one could not have ventured to expose one's uncovered head for a moment to a single ray.

I saw a new thing in this place. The ground was everywhere strewn with innumerable porcupine quills—those pretty brown and white mottled things that *fancy baskets* are made of! —and I could scarcely realise that what I had looked upon hitherto only as curiosities from a far-off country were lying at my feet in numbers.

We halted till five o'clock in the evening— dining, sleeping, reading, and talking over our future plans under the bowery shelter, and enjoying beyond words the grateful rest. At ten o'clock at night we again halted at a village called Annās, and as our guide declared openly that after *that* he did not know the way at all, we begged the chief of this village to furnish us, if possible, with a man who could take us by the shortest route to Haikota, as we were anxious to reach it the next day.   The chief was very civil, but apparently a "poor creature" in every way, not only pecuniarily, but in spirit, and seemed to think there would be great difficulty in granting our request; we pressed it urgently, however, and at last he agreed to see what he could do.

The zareeba of the village was a very small one, and as every nook within it was already occupied we were obliged to make our camp just outside, and again, as at Shariff, we had no tent pitched, intending to be up with the first streak of dawn.   I got to bed rather sooner than usual, but had a dreadfully broken night from the unceasing noises that proceeded from the huts on the other side of the hedge, where some great fête was evidently going on.

Men and boys were shouting in repeated choruses at the top of their voices, and women were singing to the accompaniments of tom-toms and shrill fifes, while dogs barked vigorously the whole time, and donkeys added to the general discordant merriment by braying loudly.   This was all subsiding, however, about two o'clock, and I had fallen into a sounder sleep than any I had been able to get before, when I was suddenly awoke by a dull thud against my bedstead, and opened my eyes to find—oh, horror!—the face of one of the very dirtiest and most repulsive-looking of the baggage camels close to my own, and I actually felt his hot breath puffing against my cheek!

The poor old creature, although hobbled, or rather tied at the knees in the manner in which all camels are secured to prevent them from straying, had shuffled itself along to my angréb, probably to search for durra, and to my alarmed imagination looked more than half-inclined to make a supper off myself. I don't know whether I shrieked—I am sure I felt inclined to; but, anyhow, some one soon came to the rescue.

This manner of securing camels by tying them at the knee is peculiar, and could only be done with very long jointed creatures. It seemed to me somewhat heartless, for I thought it must tire the poor things terribly to be kept all night long, or for many hours in the daytime, as they often are, in one position; but the drivers assured me that as it was the natural position in which they knelt they did not suffer from it. I cannot, however, say that I felt

much comforted by this bit of Hadendoa consolation. The part of the leg between the knee
and the ankle is fastened, after the camel has
knelt down, to the part of the leg above the knee,
so that it cannot rise or straighten its legs.
That they are not as a rule tied tightly, though,
was evident from the manner in which the un-
gainly old specimen I spoke of just now had
been able to make its way from some considerable distance to where I was lying. This is
the second unexpected visitor that has appeared
by my side in the middle of the night, though
I ought not to allude to pretty Flo in the same
breath with this poor beast of burden ; and yet
I would not be ungrateful to him, for how much
good service was he not daily doing us !

An hour after this little episode the whole
camp was aroused by the arrival of the new
guide, whom the chief, in spite of his apparent
feebleness, had actually procured from a neighbouring village ; and by starlight, for there was
no moon, and the day had not yet broken, we
arose, had the camels laden, got our coffee, and
were off. It was so dim, on leaving Annãs,
that we had to go very slowly, as the land was
covered with mimosas, and a path was difficult
to find among them. By and by the sun rose,

coming out of a bank of thick mist, and appearing almost unexpectedly far higher up in the heavens than we had been looking for him; but it had been getting light for some time previously, and we had had a strong suspicion that he was behind the concealing cloud.

We then trotted on, taking a few men with us, and leaving the baggage camels to follow; but before we left, the guide, who pointed out the exact direction we were to take, begged us on no account to go farther than a certain distance, as we were nearing the country of the Baza, a wild inimical tribe, who allow no strangers, under pain of death, to enter their territory; and he said that as we should have to pass below their very hills we should all need the mutual protection we could afford each other; which specially meant, I suppose, that he and the caravan would need the protection of Charlie's rifles!

About nine o'clock, after one short halt under a scraggy tree, which gave us but little shade, we passed below these hills, which form undoubtedly a fine defence to a forbidden land. They are composed of red granite, and are exceedingly rugged and very high. It would be an ugly place for an enemy to scale, and the

defending party would have a tremendous
advantage ; but we had no scaling intentions,
and only wished to be allowed to pass un-
molested at the foot.   The Baza tribe—compris-
ing, they say, about five thousand, though the
exact number is not known—are a people who
for ages have been enemies not only to all the
other Arab tribes but to Europeans also ; and,
in fact, to every outsider.

It was by these people, you may remember,
that a few years ago a Mr. Powell, his wife
and baby, with an English nurse and other
servants, were all murdered.   He tried the
experiment of passing through the country, but
none of the party ever returned from it!

Charlie told me that when *he* was here fifteen
years ago he was anxious to hunt in the Baza
territory, and asked the other Arabs if it would
not be possible to come to an understanding with
the people.   They replied that they believed
it would *not* be possible ; but he wished so
much to go that, accompanied by a few men,
he advanced to within a short distance of the
border of the country, and a party of the tribe,
who had evidently been watching their movements, came forward to meet them.

Signs were then made from afar that a conclave was desired, and that, if one on each side would advance, weapons should be mutually laid down. This was done, Charlie putting aside his rifle, and the Baza who was to speak to him laying down his spear, but placing, however, a long pole on the ground where the boundary line was supposed to exist. To this pole Charlie went up, remaining carefully on his own side of it, as the Baza did in like manner on his. A conversation by sign language then took place, for the man spoke no Arabic, and even his patois was not quite the same as that in the north of the Soudan. They perfectly understood each other, and the Baza was quite amicable. He, however, distinctly intimated, albeit with perfect politeness, that if any of the other party crossed *that* boundary they were dead men. No inducement availed to make him alter this decision, and the idea had to be given up.

All the time we were passing the hills our camel men were, or pretended to be, very much afraid. Doubtless hundreds of eyes were watching our progress, though we did not see a single man, but concealment would have been more than easy within their rocky fortress. Whether by nature or art we could not at first determine, but enormous piles of stones were heaped up in every sort of grotesque shape, not only at the foot, but half-way up the mountain. These chiefly resembled rude obelisks, citadels, and round towers, though the likeness could have been but chance, and had, on the whole, so artificial an appearance that we finally concluded they were piled there for use—to be ready, in fact, to hurl at passing caravans; and as we heard afterwards that the tribe do use stones repeatedly for this purpose, no doubt this was the intention of the heaps. The hills were interspersed with little bushes, which, when green, must look extremely beautiful.

These people possess no weapons but spears, and those only such as they have looted from vanquished enemies. They have consequently a dread of firearms, and would not be likely to attack an armed party if not actually within their land, so we kindly fired off rifles at intervals to warn them (entirely, of course, for their own sakes) to keep clear of us! The place we were passing through was not then their territory, though it had formerly belonged to them, but they have gradually been driven farther and farther back into their mountains by both Egyptians and Abyssinians, and the day is probably not remote when they will be either exterminated or conquered.

They still, however, make raids in large parties on flocks and herds grazing below in the plains in the neighbourhood of their hills, and the herdsmen, having no firearms, and seeing themselves likely to be overpowered by numbers, often fly, when some at least of the unfortunate animals under their charge are sure to fall into the hands of the enemy. We, I am glad to say, got safely past this dreaded region, and halted about noon in one of the immense pasture-lands that I long to see after the rains. It was simply a gigantic park. For miles the ground was perfectly flat, and though the grass had totally disappeared, and nothing but white dust remained, while the immense trees that were dotted all about were perfectly leafless, yet one could easily see that when all this is covered with thick turf, and the trees are green, it must be a lovely place. It was only about a mile from the river, and hundreds of cows and many flocks of goats were being driven along to a place where the water was scooped up daily out of the parched sand for them to drink. We got some milk, ate biscuits, and rested for ten minutes, but longer than that we dared not stay, for it was already getting hot beyond all endurance.

The poor dogs suffered dreadfully, even at this early hour, from scorched feet, and limped painfully, sometimes lying down and refusing to stir, and they could with difficulty be got to move on. Elfie became so ill that Charlie took him upon his camel and carried him until we reached Haikota.

Latterly it got so hot that, as we neared the town, Charlie, being encumbered with the dog, and anxious about two others that were being led by a servant, proposed to me to trot on and overtake the baggage camels that had gone ahead, rather than remain longer in the sun; but *no*, I remembered Kassala too well to consent to separate from him in going into a strange place again, and preferred to endure any amount of heat rather than ramble by myself between the party in front, who were out of sight, and the one behind, with perhaps the chance of ultimately getting away from both, so I remained where I was.

Heartily glad we both were afterwards that I had done so. Haikota was not a town, but a long straggling encampment, stretching away for a mile or more along the river-bank, and many a time we turned up a wrong alley of

birsch huts between the dôm palms, and had
to go back again, before we discovered either
the sheik's quarters or the place to which our
servants had gone.

Encamped close by, moreover, in the dry
bed of the river, were the ragged huts of two
thousand Arabs—several, in fact, of the nomad
tribes, who were wandering over the country,
and who had come there for the little water
which, with difficulty, was now to be found,
but who would be off again with the first appearance of rain; indeed, they would have to go
before it arrived, or I was told that they would
be swept out of their huts.   Finally, at noon—
having marched since four o'clock that morning
—after a good deal of search, we reached the
diwan, a miserable hut, also in the river-bed,
and found it occupied by a most odious Egyptian soldier, who is here to collect tribute, and
evidently in his own eyes a person of vast
importance,—but a horrible bully he looked.

He was asleep in this diwan, and showed the
greatest reluctance to stir, would not give us a
word of welcome, and absolutely scowled with
rage.   In we went, however, nothing daunted
by either man or scowl, feeling that the rest-
house for travellers was ours as much as his,

and off his angréb he at length dragged himself, and condescended to sit up, while I mentally pictured to myself the situation had I arrived there alone.

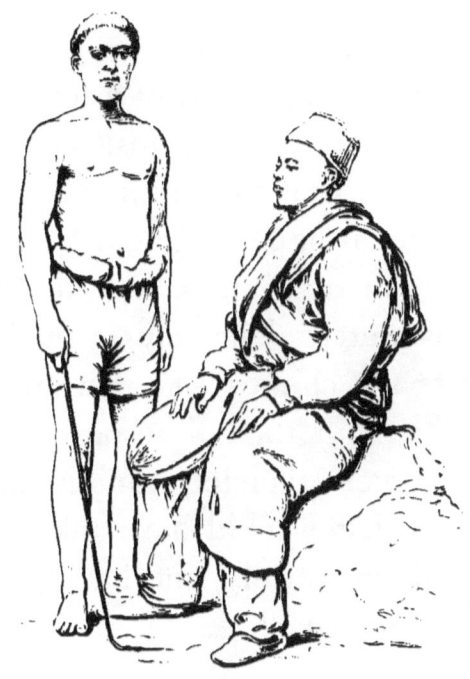

EGYPTIAN SOLDIERS COME TO COLLECT TRIBUTE.

We had scarcely dismounted when the usual swarm of darkies gathered around, coming to the front with the same marvellous rapidity that a London crowd arises on the smallest provocation, but very soon the sheik himself appeared and behaved with extreme civility. He gave us a warm welcome, declared himself ready to assist us in any way, and said that by and by, when we had rested and had had refreshment, he would return to talk with us over our plans. The soldier and the crowd took themselves off, and we were left at last in peaceful possession of the hut.

In a few minutes the gift of a fine sheep was sent up to the door for our inspection, and we knew from past experience in what form we should next see it appearing soon ! Coffee was then brought in by some dear little Arab slave boys—such pretty, delicately-formed children they were, with clothes that certainly "more expressed than hid their lithesome limbs," and dark bright eyes glancing timidly at one; I really believe that I could have taken them up and kissed them warmly, and had I been alone perhaps I might have !

LETTER XXVII.

HAIKOTA, 15*th May.*

THE heat is really too terrific to allow of my
writing much at a time, or indeed of doing anything for long together, so I must just scribble
a little bit now and then, and I trust you will
pardon the disjointed, disconnected style which
is sure to arise in consequence, and which,
indeed, I fear has been characteristic of my
epistles all through.   Sometimes my heart
almost sinks as the idea flashes across me of
what we shall have to endure before July com-
mences and the rains regularly set in,—when
we may hope that it will become a little cooler,
—but if fever only keeps off we shall struggle
along well enough, I have no doubt, after all.

Our decision about Collaláb has been unhappily unhinged by the universal voice here; and though it is really extremely difficult, as it always has been, to know whether the advice given us can be relied on, yet in the face of all that we hear we feel that we scarcely ought to risk going there. This is somewhat discomforting after the arrangements we have already made with Faki Ali, but, if what they tell us is true, my suspicions as to the integrity of that venerable counsellor were not unfounded.

It is urged that it is not only unhealthy, but that we should there be greatly troubled during the rains with that pest of Africa, the "fly," that this would necessitate sending the camels away to some other place, and that even were they able to remain with us, the whole country round Collaläb is so slushy and slimy during the rains that we should not be able to use them, as they could not move about. After endless discussions with chiefs and hunters, who have buzzed round us unceasingly, just as they did at Hamza's, each volunteering a different course, and each probably self-interested, we have decided to go to a place called Daga, on a branch of the river Barka, where we are promised immunity from every ill! According to the old proverb, we "halve and halve again

that promise," and even then feel inclined to
quarter it!—but it may be that one place, if no
worse, is as good as another, and so to Daga
we will go. While we are here, however, I
must give you a sketch of the place and our
surroundings, for I have found a strange fascination in Haikota, which is owing, I think, to the
intelligence of many of the folk here, and to
the apparently very sincere interest they take
in us and all our doings.

After we took possession of the rest-house
on the morning of our arrival, and turned out
the sulky soldier, we shook ourselves down, and
brought our palace into ship-shape, though this
was not very easy to do. The farther we wander
the more remarkable become our abodes ; and
I am thankful that in this respect we are let
down by degrees, for no one knows what we
may arrive at next.

This hut is, as the one at Hamza's zareeba
was, merely a room about fifteen feet square,
made entirely of straw ; the roof is flat, and
towards the top, especially in the corners, I see,
as before, innumerable small and unpleasing gaps.

There are, in this not very extensive domi-
cile, three doorways, which, considering its size,
appears to be a most unnecessary number, and

to only one of these is there anything whatever in the shape of a door ; the other two were on our arrival perfectly unprotected, offering free and easy access to all comers, and being thus, of course, quite open to the public view.

The hut, which is in a narrow part of the river bed, stands alone, and this is a comfort, although it is within a stone's throw of the camp of two thousand Arabs that I mentioned before, but they are fortunately on the other side of the zareeba hedge. This hedge is, however, inconveniently low—lower than any other we have yet been protected by—and one of the uncovered doorways looks over it towards the Arab camp. The other two—one of which is also a mere gap in the side of the hut—looks straight up to the chief's own special enclosure, which stands above us on the river-bank.

This enclosure consists of about a dozen little birsch houses, the occupants of which would be able to gaze down upon us in our abode all day long at their own sweet wills, did our wills also so incline. Preferring, however, a certain amount of privacy, in a manner which, I am sure, is regarded as cold-hearted and unsociable, the very first thing we did was to fasten up rugs and wrappers to this gap, arranging them by means of poles placed across, so that they could only be opened at our own desire.

Our floor is of sand, the softest and finest you can imagine, but thick and deep to an inconvenient degree, and as it is totally useless, from the swarms of white ants in the ground below, to put down any sort of matting or rug, we simply have to go without; and things are for ever getting lost by falling down and becoming buried before one is aware that they have dropped. You will think that I am exaggerating, but it is not so. In one moment a thing becomes hidden from view in this perfectly dry powdery stuff, and the very search for it often diminishes the chance of finding it. The other day I was in despair about my scissors, thinking they had gone for ever, and my signet ring I gave up for good and all, when, by the greatest good luck, it was felt, not seen, in the ever-shifting sand.

The white ants that I alluded to just now would eat us out of house and home if we gave them the chance. It was just the same in the melon garden at Kassala, and is so all over the Soudan; and the unfortunate thing is that one does not become in the least aware of them until the mischief is done. We had a sad experience of this long ago, on one of our first marches after leaving Suakin. Not dreaming that they could be so viciously disposed, or do their work so rapidly, we put down some beautiful Indian "dharries" one night, but to our consternation we found in the morning that the under side had been completely eaten away, and had they been allowed to continue down, by the evening, if then taken up, they would have almost fallen to pieces.

These horrible little creatures have scarcely any right at all to the name of "ant," for they are, in the stage in which they eat things in this terrible manner (though later on they have wings) very much like maggots, being of a soft mashy nature, with merely an ant's head and, so to speak, *shoulders ;* they are about the size of a barleycorn, and are nasty beyond everything in appearance. They always work completely in the dark, coming up out of the ground and boring into things from below, and though they undermine and sap everything, from the inside their work is never visible, as they leave the exterior of whatever they attack perfect, though it may be but a mere shell that remains. If they wish to go across an open space that is exposed to the light they fling up a tunnel of earth as they march, shutting themselves in step by step, and thus still remaining in the dark. They work with the most amazing rapidity, having been known in this way to cross a wide room in a single night, even working up the outside of the leg of a table, and down the corresponding one on the opposite side, the tunnel they left clearly indicating the route they had taken.

Every single article—boxes, bedsteads, even chairs unless frequently moved—whatever the thing may be that one wishes to preserve, has to be placed on something to raise it from the ground. Bricks or stones are best, as the ants naturally cannot work through minerals, but if these are not to be had, thick blocks of wood will answer the purpose, provided they are not allowed to remain too long in one place, in which case they too would assuredly be sacked, and whatever was upon them would become the next victim.

At Kassala, in the romantic melon garden, I was very nearly meeting with a most unromantic accident, owing to the ravages of these marauders. They had eaten their way right through the wooden leg of my bedstead, which was standing on the ground. I found it by chance one night, just as I was about to get into bed, to be perfectly hollow, and, had I not discovered the evil in time, I should, by the capsizing of the whole angréb, have been immediately turned out on to the floor, after the manner of those patent beds I have heard of, which turn their occupants out to wake them up.

16th May. We were up at five o'clock this morning photographing the Arab encampment on the river-bank as soon as early coffee was finished.   It was hard work, but great fun all the same.   The supreme difficulty, after grouping the natives, was to get them to understand that they must remain like statues.   They would change a position or an attitude over and over again just as the cap of the camera was on the very verge of coming off, and had to be shouted at, and shoved back again into the proper posture, and threatened with untold consequences if they stirred!   The first photo was a group of a dozen Arabs—picked men, all fine-looking fellows, standing, squatting, lying, in all kinds of attitudes, with the sheik in the centre, and camels and donkeys into the bargain interspersed among the men.   It was a splendid subject for a picture, but, under the circumstances, very difficult to manage as a

photograph. They were all beneath the shade
of a wide-spreading tree, where long conclaves
as to the shooting take place, and behind were
tents, dotted about under dôm palms, with other
natives squatting at the tent-doors. Nobody
was reluctant to be posed, nor afraid of the
camera as we thought they might be; but, on
the contrary, all were most amenable; indeed,
I think they enjoyed it, and felt that in some
mysterious manner they were being honoured,
although I doubt whether they really understood
what was being done, and were sorely perplexed
as to why they were to remain so still.

The donkeys and camels were led up at the
last moment when every one was placed, into
the spaces left vacant for them, and they all
behaved admirably, quite as well as their more
intelligent neighbours! The whole affair occupied us an hour and a half, and we were driven
to despair over and over again by the *contretemps* that took place, but we accomplished it
in the end, and I trust that when it is developed
it will be a success. That process, however,
will not come off until we are established at
Daga; when we shall have plenty of time, and
also be able to get rain water. We took some
photos at Kassala, but, having neither properly

distilled, nor rain water, they were alas! a failure. After this we formed another group consisting of the sheik, reclining on an impromptu divan, made by throwing a large rug over an angréb and arranging pillows and

SHEIK, ADAM, AND PRIEST.

cushions round it, with an old hunter called Adam on a gorgeous mat at his feet, and a most remarkable-looking old gaunt priest in the background. The surroundings were the same as before, the group being under the large tree; but this time no one else was included, and there was consequently far less difficulty in managing the picture. This also was a fine subject, and would have made a beautiful painting, with the brilliant yet subdued lights that fell athwart, penetrating through the deep shade of the palms overhead.

Then we took Adam alone, and the sheik also by himself. He, too, is a fine man, and such a good fellow that I must tell you about him by and by.

When the photographing was over he wished to be initiated into the mysteries of the camera, so we exhibited them to him and a few of the more intelligent of the men, who were exceedingly anxious to know what was the result that had been achieved, and, indeed, what it was that had been done with them. Hastily posing a few people, we called the spectators by turns up to the camera ; but there was the greatest difficulty in making them see anything at all ! Perplexed and amazed, they declared at first that there was "nothing there." Suddenly, however, the sheik caught sight of the group which was patiently waiting for his inspection, and his amazement and delight knew no bounds, and after a short time the efforts of the others were also successful. Positive screams of delight, accompanied by roars of laughter, issued from Adam when a passing figure threw an unexpected apparition of huge dimensions on the glass ; but I believe the whole party thought the affair supernatural from beginning to end, and were decidedly more in awe of the camera after they had looked into the mysterious depths of that small cavity than they had been before.

19th May. A few mornings ago, as we were having coffee outside the hut, about six o'clock, the sheik came up and, after the usual salutations, asked very politely whether we would like to see a parade of his Beni-Amer horsemen —his little troop, of whom he is justly proud. We were of course delighted at the proposition, though we little imagined what we were about to see, and in a few minutes accompanied him to the spot where they were all drawn up. The news of the coming inspection had spread not only through the whole village of Haikota but also through the nomad encampment, and almost every one turned out to witness the performance. Our own surprise and pleasure consisted, however, not so much in the manœuvres, which though spirited were not extraordinary, but in the accoutrements of the soldiers and horses. There were about fifty riders all wearing chain armour, identically the same as that used of old by the crusaders!

The horses had thickly-padded coverings, of the same pattern that one has seen as belonging to olden times, made of Arab cloth; and one proof that they were not modern was, that they were far too large and long for the horses that were wearing them.   There was no doubt that they had not been made for them, but for war-horses of a nobler height and build.

We inquired eagerly as to how these suits of armour had come into the possession of the tribe, and from whom they had been handed down; but to these questions we could obtain no satisfactory answers, the only reply being that they were heirlooms from unknown ages; and they were, we were glad to find, looked upon as intensely valuable and most highly prized.

No inducements would persuade the sheik to part with a single suit, though we were excessively anxious to take one home; and seeing, after a time, how much he really prized them we desisted from our entreaties, and con-fined our observations to admiration only.

The favourite display of horsemanship seemed to be to gallop round and round an immense circle at full speed, and, at a moment's notice, rein in the horses without previously checking them. This was done many times,—to the greater satisfaction of the riders than the ridden, it seemed to me,—though I did not volunteer the observation.

After the cavalry parade they showed us how their infantry fight, their only weapons being spear and shield, and with these they exhibited attack and defence.

At the commencement of every manœuvre, whether from the mounted or foot soldiers, all the women among the bystanders, several hundred in number, raised a peculiar shrill cry which is most remarkable, and, coming without warning, was somewhat startling. The same custom, I am told, is prevalent in Abyssinia, and is called the "El-elta," or cry of victory. They place their hands in a curved position in front of their mouths, forming a sort of hollow tube, and draw their tongues with the most amazing rapidity backwards and forwards—a very difficult movement to attain proficiency in—which assists them to produce a shrill trilling sound.

At the conclusion of the whole performance we photographed some of the horsemen, taking four groups which gave every appearance of being likely to turn out successful.[1]

[1] In consequence of an accident, which most unfortunately occurred on the journey home, the negatives of most of our photographs got broken, so that it was impossible to reproduce them ; and those which escaped were so injured that they were almost unfit for use.

LETTER XXVIII.

HAIKOTA, 24*th May*.

BEFORE we leave Haikota I must tell you of
some of the shooting expeditions that have taken
place, for they have been full of interest, though
not so successful as could have been wished.

There is no doubt whatever that there is
far less game in the Soudan now, and that what
there is, is much more difficult to get than it
was formerly. The fatigue, moreover, of shooting in this season proves to be too intense to
make it feasible as a continuance, for any one
but natives.

The whole of this part of Africa is now so very
much more densely populated than it has ever
been before, and the Arabs themselves shoot so

much more than they did, that the animals retire
farther and farther into the dense jungles, and
when they are driven near the abodes of men by
stress of thirst in the hot weather they are so
extremely wary that obtaining them is almost
impossible.   With regard to elephants there
seems to be little doubt that the natives are very
reluctant that Europeans should ever get them.
Finding the ivory trade valuable they throw ob-
stacles in the way of other hunters, and we have
had reason to fear that on more than one occasion
treachery of this kind has spoiled the sport.

The very evening of our arrival Charlie went
over to the sheik's camp and sat under the big
tree I mentioned before for more than a couple
of hours, discussing with him and several hunters
the best localities for game and the best methods
of obtaining it, while the usual crowd of at least
fifty followers surrounded the select group.

The hunter whom I spoke of in my last letter,
called Adam, is a real old patriarch in appearance.   He seemed so reliable at first that we
could not but believe in him, and thought he was
the very "soul of honour."   Alas! before long
we began to fear that he was not quite all we
had imagined, though his appearance was even
then so much in his favour that it was a con-

siderable time before we could make up our minds really to doubt him.

He is one of the sword-hunters of the Hamran Arabs, and a fine specimen of the race. Not very tall, indeed rather under the usual

ADAM.

height, but wiry and strong, with every muscle well knit together, and still, though not a young man, extremely active.

He has fine eyes and good features, and a weather-beaten face that tells its own tale of years of hard forest toil and outdoor life, with an expression full of intelligence and keenness (perhaps it is a little too keen!), in which, although I have lost the faith I had in him, I even still think that kindness and benevolence mingle.

The variety of advice and opinion that was offered under the tree that evening as to the best direction for finding elephants was so endless that no conclusion was arrived at, especially as the terms demanded by most of the hunters were so exorbitant that it would have been folly to comply with them. Time and the judicious encouragement of competition were needed to reduce them to reasonable dimensions.

The diplomacy by which Adam had tried to obtain his price was of a curious character, but proved in the end a total failure. He had endeavoured to show the invaluable nature of his services by saying that *remuneration was nothing to him!* Yet *his* charges were higher than any of the others! For himself he wished to hunt no more; but on this occasion, as a special favour, he would make an exception. He boasted of having killed hundreds of elephants in his day, and of having amassed thousands of dollars, and he said he now desired no further gain. Feeling that if any work were to be got out of him it would be well to nip this bombast

in the bud, Charlie, after listening to the story
of his riches, quietly asked him where then was
his house, where his horses, his servants, and
why he was not clothed in magnificent robes
and covered with gold ornaments after the
manner of the wealthy in the East.

He shuffled a little to one side uneasily,
spread out his hands, palms uppermost, with an
à quoi bon gesture, and replied that "that was
not the custom of his particular tribe."   The
bystanders laughed in a manner that expressed
volumes, and Adam moved away from the
group.   At that juncture another hunter came
forward with wholly different propositions.   To
begin with, he wished to transport our whole
camp across the Gāsh again (we having only
just arrived at Haikota!) to a distant part of
the country, where he declared there was much
more game.

With no intention whatever of acceding to
this, but for the sake of seeing whether in spite
of Adam's disinterested protestations his terms
would not abate, this man was encouraged,
and an arrangement was to all appearance on
the verge of being made with him when Adam,
who had taken care to be the whole time within
earshot, came to the front again.

He sauntered carelessly up as though he had returned merely by accident, and, seating himself on the ground at Charlie's feet, commenced making other propositions. He had been brought to the ground in more senses than one! Then very gradually, and after almost as long a time as had been already spent, with a wily show of infinite reluctance to listen to him at all, an agreement was arrived at, and the other man was told that the Gāsh must be tried first, for we could not again move so immediately. The next day the plans for the first expedition took a definite shape. It was arranged that at three o'clock the following morning Adam should show the way to a place where he said he believed it was likely elephants might be found. They were to go to the springs at which they would probably have drunk during the night, and, taking up the tracks at daybreak, follow them till they traced the animals to their hiding-places in the forest. This programme was carried out.

The party consisted of Charlie, Adam, and two of Adam's trackers on horseback, with six others on foot, three camels, one for water and the other two for carrying food and such things as were required, and also for bringing

home the spoil which it was fondly hoped they
might return with.   Adam's trackers were men
who were always employed by him, but who
were now with him engaged for special service
during this fortnight.   The others were our
own servants and employés, with whom Adam
had nothing to do.   I mention this because by
and by I shall have to speak more particularly
of them all.

It was not unlikely that the party would
remain out, not only that day but the following
night too, for if they did not find the elephants
in the forest they would return to the water
and watch for them there ; or, as it was not
usual for elephants to drink two consecutive
nights at the same place, they might deem it
best to go to the next springs, which were a
great distance off.

After riding for about eighteen miles over a
plain, covered so thickly with thorny mimosas
that speed was impossible, they came to a
jungle too dense for the camels to enter, so,
leaving them, they took one of the smaller
water-skins, which was slung to one of the
horses.   They then made the best of their way,
in and out among thorns, for another six miles,
till they came to a part of the forest which the

horses even could not go through ; so, here
dismounting, they crawled on hands and knees
through a thicket of the thorniest of all the
thorny bushes of Africa, the "kittar." Footmarks of elephants had been clearly visible
the whole way, so in spite of getting clothes
terribly torn, and hands and faces cruelly
lacerated, the sportsmen were ever allured
onwards, and at last they had their reward.
On the border of the densest bit of jungle they
had yet come to, in a small space that happened
to be tolerably clear, about sixty yards in front,
were an immense bull elephant, a female, and a
little one.

All were asleep ; the huge parents were
standing side by side, bolt upright, facing them,
and the little one was lying down. Charlie took
a steady aim and fired ; but, though he hit the
male with a bullet from an eight-bore rifle right
in the middle of the forehead, to his intense
chagrin the enormous creature, instead of drop-
ping, instantly turned and ran, and there was
not even time for a second shot, or at any rate
for one that could have reached a vital part.
The other barrel was, however, immediately
levelled at the female, which also had tusks,
and the contents hit her in the shoulder as she

also turned.   It was hoped that the bullet might penetrate the heart, but her rapid movement frustrated this, and she bolted as quickly as the bull, following him into the seemingly impenetrable bush, and the little one was gone too as rapidly as the others ; *that* was another disappointment, as they had hoped to take it alive.

In spite of the terrible jungle, the hunters managed to follow the fugitives for about a couple of miles, but were then obliged to give in and return to the camp, their small supply of water not allowing them to go farther, and it was impossible to tell to what distance the animals might not have run.   The heat was terrific, even the natives suffered terribly, and Charlie was very much exhausted.

The disappointment of losing this pair was extreme, for the male especially would have been a magnificent prize.   He was a splendid animal, over ten feet in height, and each tusk was at least five feet in length.   This circumstance, however, confirmed Charlie's former opinion that an African elephant will not drop from a head wound unless hit by a bullet twice the size of that he had then with him.   His rifles, when he was in this same part of the

world and in Abyssinia fifteen years ago, were
much larger, and he was then repeatedly successful, but, as meanwhile this very rifle has
killed elephants both in India and the Malay
Straits, he thought he would try it now in Africa.
Had the elephants charged, dangerous as it
would have been, they might yet perhaps have
been killed, but the Gāsh elephants, we are told,
never charge, they always run.

It seemed so grievous that these fine elephants, after having been wounded, should go
away merely to die in the jungle, that a consultation took place that afternoon as to the best
means of finding them. Adam's opinion was that
if badly hurt they would return to the river
the same night to drink, and perhaps lie down
there to die ; but if the wounds were not severe
they would probably have gone a great distance ;
nevertheless, he thought they could possibly be
traced. As, however, they did not come to the
river that night, a large party of men were sent
out the following morning as soon as it was
light, who tracked the trio up for miles, distinctly
following their footmarks all the way ; but they
at last decided that they must have gone to the
Settit, nearly a hundred miles off, and that there
was therefore no possibility of getting them.

Nothing daunted, however, Charlie was out again the next night with Adam and several trackers to watch till daybreak at the springs, hoping that other elephants would come to drink, but nothing appeared. This, however, we were more than half inclined to think was owing to an action on Adam's part, which at the time appeared inexplicable, but which may have had a meaning known only to himself. After spending several hours in almost breathless silence, and with every nerve at the utmost tension, listening for the slightest sound that might give indication of an approach, Adam, without any warning, suddenly fired, and to Charlie's amazement, when he went up to see what had fallen, it was only a hyena! Naturally enough, he was excessively angry with Adam, who stammered forth that he had mistaken it for a lion; but there was not much probability of such a skilled old hunter being deceived in this way, and the greater likelihood was that his practised ear had heard elephants approaching, and, wishing to reserve them for himself another day, he had given them this timely warning of enemies at hand.

Of course after this it was useless to watch any longer. Every beast of the forest for miles round, directly the shot was fired, would have instantly betaken itself in the opposite direction; and perplexed, indignant, and sorely vexed, the Khawajah at once ordered a return to the camp.

Shortly after this another circumstance occurred which tended still farther to shake our faith in Adam. One of our own men came mysteriously to the hut one morning as soon as we were astir, and begged to be allowed a private interview. With bated breath, glancing constantly over his shoulder, and speaking in a tone hardly audible, he said that they had reason to distrust Adam and his men. Another man, who was too timid to come up, had overheard Adam's trackers saying to each other the day before, in *sotto voce* tones, that they believed they would yet find the first elephant that had been shot. On hearing this, which was confirmed by several of our servants, Charlie at once determined on another expedition himself in search of it, and ordered the camels to be got ready immediately for a three or four days' tour, resolving either to follow up the old tracks until successful, or to go elsewhere when once started. Adam was not informed of the immediate design of the expedition lest he should in some way circumvent it, but he was merely ordered to attend. For the first time he looked sulky, dogged, and extremely angry, and had he known the real object in view he would probably have looked darker still.

They went out for several miles in the former direction till they reached a place called in the Bijjia language "*Ooah Okrub*," the elephant-rock. Seeing, however, that in spite of its name there was not much likelihood of finding any game there in broad daylight, the situation being too exposed, they went on to Bārā Bārā, "the place of screens," the screens being high rocks that formed a good shelter. Here they met by chance an Abyssinian hunter, who had known Charlie in Abyssinia as "Basha Felika" in former years. The man recognised him, gave him a warm greeting, and advised him, instead of pursuing former elephants, to remain in that neighbourhood for the night, saying that hiding-places should be made for himself and Adam at some distance from each other, so that each might have a chance, as elephants would very likely pass that spot in going down to the river for water.

This was determined upon, and a man was

sent back to the camp with a few words scrawled
in pencil on the back of an old envelope to tell
me to send off a spade, a pick-axe, and some
hatchets. I despatched the things, and felt
more than half inclined to go myself and watch
also at the "place of screens," but refrained,
thinking that, in case of such a pursuit as the
former one being necessary, I *might* perhaps
hinder the success!

Hiding-places are frequently made by the
natives when watching for game; they dig
holes in the ground, in which they squat, sufficiently wide to admit of their bringing a rifle
to the shoulder, but allowing only their heads
to come above the surface of the ground.

Over the top, to hide their heads, they
arrange the jungle, pulling down the branches
in a thick mass as nearly like the surrounding
thicket as they can make it; and in these exca-
vations they lie in ambush the whole night long,
waiting with untiring patience for their prey.
Two places of concealment of this sort were
made that day, about the distance of a quarter
of a mile apart—one for the Khawajah, the
other for Adam—and in them they respectively
stationed themselves.

This having all been arranged, a large party

of our own trackers and servants were sent off in the direction in which the other longed-for elephants had escaped, and great hopes were entertained that one or other of these fresh efforts might turn out successful.

Hour after hour went by with the watchers, and nothing had come in Charlie's way, when, to his surprise, he heard a shot from Adam's quarter, and running over to see what had happened, found that he had actually got a fine bull elephant. Two large tuskers together had come to within twenty yards of his ambuscade, and in an over-cautious moment, before moving on to the water, had stood perfectly still to reconnoitre. Doubtless some faint suspicion had crossed their keen instincts that all was not right, and, while standing with heads erect and ears slightly bent forward on the *qui vive* for any definite warning, a steel-tipped bullet had sped with unerring aim and pierced the lungs of one of the two, having, as was afterwards discovered, completely shattered them. The huge creature had even then bolted about a hundred yards into the jungle, but there dropped dead, while his friend had made off at the first sound of the rifle, and had wholly disappeared. When morning dawned, instead of coming home (home to the Haikota hut!) the hunters set out in the opposite direction to follow the party who had gone the day before in search of the other elephants, and about noon met them returning. The spoor had been traced for miles, but at last unfortunately lost, having become obliterated by rain which had fallen in that part of the country.

The previous night having proved so successful, one more was now determined upon at the " place of screens," and the party returned to the jungle, the sportsmen taking up their stations as before in their places of concealment.

From ten o'clock till two they waited and watched, weary but wakeful. Two of Charlie's trackers who were with him had both at last lain down beneath the concealing branches, and, stretched flat upon the ground, were fast asleep. The night was not favourable ; the moon, which was waning, had only just risen, and clouds were sweeping across, obscuring the little light there was. Suddenly, in the dim fitfulness, a large dark object, " like a massive column," moved slowly and silently along, about a hundred and fifty yards off, in the direction of the spring. At first it was impossible to distinguish even what it was, but suddenly for a moment the clouds drifted away, and the huge form of a fine tusker was clearly displayed. This was evidently the friend of the one which had been shot the previous night, now without doubt, returning to look for him. He lifted his huge head in the air, waved his trunk backwards and forwards for a second, evidently sniffed the carcase of his departed comrade, and, becoming convinced of his fate, turned with amazing swiftness and fled into the jungle. He had been too restless the whole time, and the light had been too uncertain, to admit of a shot, and so he escaped.

Still the watchers did not stir till six o'clock, when, wearied out with the unceasing fatigue and continual watchfulness of the preceding forty-eight hours, they got up and came home. About eleven o'clock they entered the camp, and the camels, bringing the elephant meat and the heavy tusks, followed soon after. The sight that the zareeba hedge presented for the next few days was one you would scarcely have liked to see. Strips of meat were spread out in every direction to dry in the sun,—in fact, it was a drying-ground of elephant meat,—and this was of necessity for the most part near the servants' quarters, and a great deal of it was much nearer *our* quarters than was agreeable, for if we had not watched it the two thousand Arabs encamped within the distance of a stone's throw would have very soon known better than any one else where it all went to. It was to be dried and then stacked as the hippo meat had been, and was to be the *pièce de resistance* to serve servants, and trackers, and dogs for many a long day. But oh, meanwhile, how one's nostrils suffered! At lunch-time, as a delicate attention, Sher Ullah brought in a tureen full of soup made from it, but no sooner had it entered the doorway than I screamed out for it to be taken away again. Whatever it might be when the meat was dried, I could not bear it *then*, and I think you would have said so too if it had been offered you. I cannot describe it. It was *too* dreadful.

One more shooting expedition I must relate, because it brought to light several curious manners and customs of these fine creatures, whom in my heart I cannot help feeling very sorry for. The Arabs hunt them unceasingly and without mercy, and in time there is very little doubt that in all the thickly-inhabited parts of Africa they will be entirely exterminated.

The same party as usual went out one night

and halted near some wells about five miles off. About midnight a large herd came down to drink, stealthily creeping over the sand almost without a sound. I must give you the description in the words that I wrote down as Charlie told me of it. He said : " I saw the enormous creatures, their huge size appearing magnified by the moonlight, creeping silently along like ghosts ; they were almost absolutely noiseless, but vigilant as hares, turning their big heads constantly in every direction, and often stopping to listen at the slightest chance sound that occurred. There was not a breath stirring, and all that was to be heard was the occasional fall of a dead leaf or the crackling of a branch. There were four very fine tuskers in the herd, and five or six females, also with tusks, and one young one. The whole party, with the exception of one male, advanced to the wells, and I could not help noticing that *the females were allowed to drink first*, while the males kept watch. One male, that had not gone with the others to the water, had evidently been told off for sentry duty on a more extensive scale. In the same stealthy manner in which the whole herd had advanced, he proceeded to

make a wide circuit in the surrounding neighbourhood, and, after a thorough reconnoitre,
drew himself up within fifty yards of our
hiding-place, presenting an unsuspicious and
magnificent front to our admiring gaze. Here
was the very opportunity I had longed for;
scarcely would such a chance occur again in
a hundred times. I instantly touched Adam,
who was by me, lightly on the arm as a signal
for him to cock his rifle and be in readiness
when I had fired, as we had agreed upon
beforehand. I then raised my rifle, and took
a deliberate aim; the ball penetrated the elephant's chest, it staggered, and we both believed
it would fall on the spot, when to our unutterable amazement, as the others had done
before it, it also turned and was gone in a
moment. The whole herd had also vanished
at the sound of the shot, and of all the number
there had been on the ground a minute before
not one was now left." They went away with
such rapidity that even the wounded one could
not be found, though they were tracked for
miles, but Adam said he was sure it would
die as it had been too badly hit to live long,
and he did not despair of getting it the next
night, but this hope, alas, was not fulfilled!

LETTER XXIX.

Preliminary downpours—Washed out—We pack up hastily—
Storm passes off—Unpacked and unrolled—The storm
comes on in earnest—The river rises—Two feet of water
sweeping wildly past—Everything floating—The sheik's
birsch house—I describe water-pipes—Servants roar with
laughter—The tent a "slough of despond"—Lovely night
—We decide to move at once.

HAIKOTA, 26th May.

I BELIEVE we shall be off to-morrow for Daga,
but if it were not for a disastrous termination
to our stay here, in the shape of a flood, which
washed us out of our hut, and has made everything so uncomfortable that it has quite changed
the aspect of things, I should be really sorry to
go, for in many ways I have greatly enjoyed
my sojourn here.

This flood has warned us, however, that the
rains are near at hand; there seems to be a
likelihood of their commencing this year earlier
than usual, and we feel anxious to be settled
before they really begin. Preliminary down-

pours of the kind we had last night often come at intervals and partially before the wet season sets in for good ; and it was a *shower* of this sort that obliterated the footmarks of the elephants that our trackers went out to look for ten days ago. I have seen the rains in India, and the rains in the Malay peninsula, but from the mere trifle that nearly drowned us yesterday I would rather *not* see the coming rains of Africa, and fate defend us (or any unfortunate mortals) from being exposed to them !

I will describe what happened when we were " washed out." We were sitting two days ago —about five o'clock in the evening, as we often did at that time—outside our hut, and were showing the sheik and Adam the illustrations in Sir Samuel Baker's *Nile Tributaries*. They were immensely interested, and Adam was particularly quick at discovering the animals in the pictures. Suddenly, without any warning, a gale arose all in a moment, like a whirlwind, almost taking my breath away, and hurling sand and dust in blinding confusion all around. We all looked up in consternation, and the sheik said it would probably pour in torrents almost immediately, and that it was evidently raining hard in the hills in Abyssinia—the outline of

which we could see in the distance covered
with clouds as black as ink.   He advised
that we should have the tent pitched at once
upon the bank, for he said the river-bed would
be flooded in half an hour; and he shouted for
men to come and assist, though the hurricane
was so terrific he could scarcely make his
voice heard at all.   Several of his people,
however, came running down of their own
accord, thinking we should be in need, and
while they all went to put up the tent Sher
Ullah and I hurried into the hut to pack up
everything, so as to have the boxes carried
to the high ground where the flood would
not reach them.   Not a moment was to be
lost; there was no time for either reflection
or selection; things had to be stuffed in and
rammed down just as they would go, and the
lids banged to with kicks and blows, and the
keys turned in the locks, without thinking
about where any special thing was put, or
how we were ever to find it again.   Then
the bedding was hastily rolled up and en-
closed in the protecting ox-hides, and the
angrébs were turned up on end, and all was
ready in a jiffy for the men's shoulders.   I
never equalled that packing (if "packing" it

could be called) for rapidity, and yet I have packed a good deal in my time now and again. Just as everything was completed Charlie came in to say it was utterly impossible to pitch the tent; it had been blown out of their hands over and over again, and they had been obliged to give up the attempt. He also said that there seemed to be a likelihood of the storm passing over.

After all my haste, and the perfect state of preparation we were in for a move, I could not help feeling for a moment almost disappointed! but remembering that if the rain did come we should have no place of our own to go into, I reflected that perhaps it was as well that it should *not*. There would have been nothing for it but to ask the sheik to take us in with the mixed multitude of his numerous family to one of the birsch huts; and we did not altogether relish *that* idea. To our consternation, however, more drops fell; faster and faster they came, and the holes in the roof began to leak; still there was no flood outside, and the wind continued so very high that it seemed likely after all that the clouds would be driven away. There was, nevertheless, just enough rain falling through that leaky roof to be very unpleasant ; so while we were in doubt, hoping that we should not be obliged after all to appeal to the hospitality of the sheik, we put up umbrellas inside the hut and sat disconsolately under them, perched like two huge crows on the tops of some boxes ; and I know we presented a most ridiculous spectacle. As it was almost quite dark Sher Ullah lighted a small hand - lantern there happened to be at hand — the gale being too great for him to bring in either lamps or candles from his own shed, where they were always kept—and put it down in one corner, which was safe from the drippings. It shed just light enough for us to see each other, and we could not but laugh at our mutual appearance. Soon, however, it became evident that we were not to be washed out that night ; the gale went down, the clouds had been swept away by the wind, and about nine o'clock all was as calm as possible, and quite fine. We unpacked and unrolled again, shook ourselves and our belongings as free of dust as we could get them in a short space of time—hours would have been required to do it properly—and had a cold supper, for there was no time to cook anything. The next morning everything was as glorious as usual. The sun was hotter than ever, every sign of rain, either past, present, or future, had entirely disappeared, and the sheik gave it as his opinion that, as the storm had so completely passed over, it would not come now for a considerable time—probably not until the rains began, perhaps a month hence.

We went on tranquilly in this feeling of happy security all day, until very nearly the same hour as on the previous evening; when again quite suddenly, with only a slight breeze blowing, a few heavy raindrops fell, the clouds seemed to come up as if by magic, and we clearly saw that the storm that had threatened us the night before was coming in earnest now. Charlie and the sheik and all the servants rushed away immediately, and got up the tent; it is a heavy affair, and takes a good time to pitch, and many people to do it; so they had to work hard.

Meanwhile Sher Ullah and I made our utmost speed as before in the hut, and worked away with all our might; but this time the storm did not give us half a chance—we were to suffer for not having taken his warning; but then he had acted so deceitfully during the day that we were scarcely to blame; and again, even

this night, he was treacherous! While we were
in the midst of our work all again seemed to
subside, the breeze fell, and we hesitated in our
labours.   All at once came a *burst ;* the *racuba*[1]
leaked in every direction, streams poured in on
all sides, one knew not where to turn first, or
what to lay hands on, and the darkness, which
suddenly gathered, rendered it almost impossible to know what one was doing.   The bedding was the first thing to save ; if that were
soaked where should we be for the night? so
we secured it as best we could, and we were
just beginning with the other things, when
Charlie came in soaked to the skin.   He
stopped for nothing, but, exhorting us to use
even greater speed if possible than before,
commenced helping at once, " lest," as he said,
" everything should be washed away."

I could not comprehend how such a thing
could be, and not half understanding the situation, which the experience of floods in Abyssinia
made *him* acquainted with, thought only of the
rain.   He had scarcely spoken when we heard
voices outside exclaiming that the " river was
rising," and he ran out to see.   The sheik and

[1] The particular kind of straw hut in which we had been
living.

a dozen men were there, and without waiting
for permission darted in and seized whatever
they could lay their hands on; boxes, bags,
rifles, clothes, rolls of bedding, lamps, anything
and everything was conveyed away with light-

FLOOD ON THE GĀSH.

ning speed. The scene of confusion baffles all
description. Men jabbering, sheik directing,
nobody listening, but, what was far better, everybody *working;* while about two feet of water
was sweeping wildly past, making its way into
the hut through every crack and cranny; and,
worse than all, threatening to undermine the

already unsteady posts, and bring the whole thing down upon our heads with a crash!

Before I knew where I was I found myself in Charlie's arms, every possession belonging to me left behind in the keeping of the natives, and felt that he was wading away with me across the flood, and struggling up the slippery bank, all slushy and muddy, to the sheik's birsch house, where, after all, I was to wait until goods and chattels had been conveyed into the tent.

And what had I seen as we waded through the river! If it was wild confusion inside the racuba it was still more wild outside! The cooking-pots and all the servants' things were floating, and the corn was getting soaked; but far worse than that, our dogs and donkeys, poor things,—that were tethered just at the edge of the bank,— were howling and screeching in terror, and pulling hard at their chains. The bewildered servants had utterly forgotten them, and the wind, which had risen to a gale, had prevented any one from hearing them.

Charlie put me down upon the bank, and ran for men to come and assist, for each animal, when freed, had to be held firmly by its chain, or in its fright would have bolted into the

jungle and been probably eaten during the
night by hyenas or lions.   They were all got
into safety and shelter beside the tent at the top
of the rising ground above, and we were then
conducted by the sheik to his house.

I shall never forget that walk, short as the
distance was, not above a hundred yards, for I
thought I should never get there.   The surface
of the ground, which had been baked to a dry
brittle crust, scarcely thicker than an oatmeal
biscuit, was now one mass of slime ; it was two
steps forward and one back the whole way, and
if I had not been firmly held up I believe I
should have fallen over and over again.

At last we arrived at the dwelling hospitably
placed at my disposal by the good-hearted sheik,
of whom, for that and many other kindnesses, I
shall always think with gratitude and pleasure.
It had been entirely cleared of its usual inhabitants for my reception, and, save a couple of
servants—who were ordered to seat themselves
just within the door, and to take any message
that I might wish to send, or to bring me anything I wanted—nobody was there.

Entering was not easy, the little aperture
left for that purpose being so close to the ground
that I had almost to crawl in order to get in.

From a distance I had often watched the people popping in and out of these little holes, and they had always looked to me just like rabbits darting backwards and forwards; but I now appreciated the suppleness of their limbs as I had not done before.

I had got pretty well soaked in the transit from the hut, but there was no redress for that grievance yet awhile; and the probability was that before there would be I should be perfectly dry again. After seeing me in safety, and committing me to the care of the two darkies, my pioneers disappeared again to rush back to the general rescue. After sitting for a moment or two in silence I thought I could not do better than improve the occasion by endeavouring to enter into conversation. Water being an appropriate subject that night, I described how in our houses in England it was carried up to any height in pipes, telling my hearers, in the first place, how our houses consisted of many stories, and I also tried to give them some faint idea of what doors and windows meant.

For a considerable time they listened in absolute silence with eyes fixed upon me, but uttering not a word, and I was beginning to think that my Arabic was a dead failure, and they had not understood a syllable, till I got to the history of water going up a height. Then I had most satisfactory evidence of having been quite intelligible, for the merry burst of laughter that greeted me showed that they had seized the whole situation, and, as Faki Ali had done at Kassala, they without doubt put me down in their minds as gifted with a special talent for rodomontade. About eleven o'clock Charlie came back for me, saying that the tent was ready, though he judiciously added, by way of preparation, "it is not as nice as I could wish it to be."

"Nice!" Could any single letter of the word be applied to what I beheld when after a second slippery journey, even worse than the first, I reached it? There was nothing to do but make a joke of the situation, for it was beyond quarrelling with, or even trying to rectify, *that* night; both would have been equally useless. The ground inside the tent was as wet as outside. When the storm had come on there was no possibility in the hurry and confusion of finding a spade to dig a trench, and the water had poured in from the sides underneath the canvas; and the men, in bringing in the things, had trodden it all about until it was an absolute "slough of despond." I came to anchor on a chair, from which I somehow crawled on to my bedstead (having dried again, as I anticipated I should), while Charlie, who had found a hoe at last, went out with it in one hand and a lantern in the other, to try to make a ditch to let out some of the pools, and to prevent fresh water from getting in.

Just as he was making a capital commencement the handle of the hoe broke short off, in the midst, and there was an end of *that* effort. In a short time the good devoted servants actually managed to bring up something for us to eat. I wondered then, as I have many a time besides, if *I* were a servant whether I should look as faithfully after the comfort of my masters as my own attendants do after mine; and I came, alas! to no *satisfactory* conclusion on that score. They had managed to save some chicken curry from the general wreck. Of course it was cold, and the gravy was full of ditch water, but we ate it ravenously, drank up a bottle of Medoc, and slept soundly till two o'clock. I was then awakened by some one stirring in the tent, but found, to my relief, that it was only Charlie, who was going out to slacken the ropes, which had been drawn by the wet to a dangerous tension.

The night was as calm and sweet as a night could be. The moon shone down upon us with a placid countenance that seemed almost derisive, and one could scarcely believe, in spite of the dire confusion in the tent, which her bright beams partially revealed, that the circumstances of a few hours before had not been merely an uncomfortable nightmare. As the slush in the tent dried up it took the form of hard clotted masses, and was almost like a ploughed field, and everything was steaming. A Scotch plaid that had fallen to the ground during the night, and lain there unseen for some hours, was perfectly hot and steaming too, when taken up.

About seven o'clock in the morning we went outside the tent for coffee and biscuits, and had a great confabulation afterwards with the sheik and Adam as to the advisability of remaining yet longer at Haikota or going at once to Daga, and it was finally decided that we should go at once.

Adam said, and the sheik confirmed this, that the country round the Gāsh is all so slushy during the rains that, as at Collalāb, camels would be of no use there. We were obliged to stay through yesterday, however, to dry the tent and all the other things before they could be packed, but if the sheik fulfils his promise we shall have camels to-morrow and be off as early as possible.

LETTER XXX.

DAGA, 30*th May*.

WE reached Daga, on the river Bārka, this
morning, after a three days' march from Haikota.
All our travelling was done at night, and by
day we halted, living under bowers cut out of
thick tangled masses of shrubs, with great
ox-hides hung up over the thin places to keep
off even the broken bits of sunlight. We gave
up going back to Kassala, as it would have been
out of our way to Daga, and sent camels for
the baggage, which we expect to arrive shortly.

Our exit from Haikota was quite a triumphal procession! We were escorted by the sheik, all the hunters, and half the population, who came out in grand style to do us honour! We had become quite fond of them all, and even felt inclined at the last to forgive Adam his many sins, and to doubt whether we had not ourselves been mistaken in him. Even the sulky soldier turned out with the rest, and the sheik provided three horsemen as an escort, and sent his own nephew also to show us the road, promising to follow himself in a few days.

At the last moment we were much perplexed at receiving a huge goat as a parting gift from the *sheikess*. It was difficult at this eleventh hour to know what in the world to do with it; but it was, I believe, driven along by the side of the baggage camels to the next camping-ground, after which we inquired no more as to its history. This sheik, who had been so friendly at Haikota, and who had persuaded us to come here, is Sheik Hamed, of the Beni-Amer Arabs. His brother, Mohamed Wad Jeil, is the real head of the whole Hamran country, in whose favour Hamed had waived the supreme title, "Sheik Mo Shakh" (sheik of sheiks), which had been offered him some years before. Sheik Hamed, however, though his brother wears the honours, has the greater vigour of character of the two, and, in fact, really carries stronger influence in the tribe, bearing a good name and being liked by all.   He has

SHEIK HAMED.

been always faithful to the Khedive, acknowledging Egyptian authority, and keeping his Beni-Amer men faithful too.   We had, personally, a great proof of his goodwill and friendship by his providing us with twenty-three of his own camels for the march, and he would not hear of our prepaying the drivers, doing it, on the contrary, himself, and saying we would settle all accounts later on at Daga. Meantime, by his order, houses had been vacated and prepared for us here, and we are in possession of a thick grass dwelling called a " tukul bête," which is equal to keeping out any storm of either wind or rain.

This dwelling consists of three good-sized rooms, and, except those at El Gwaiya built by our German friends, is by far the best we have yet seen. The rooms all lead one into the other, the two outer being square, the inner one circular. This third room is, in fact, a beehive-shaped hut, with two little tiny openings for windows, each only about four inches square, cut in the upright bit of grass wall which supports the pointed roof. The whole place has been thoroughly swept out and brushed down, and several inches of fine white sand have been spread all over the floors, so that it is as clean as possible.

I shall not give you a minute description of our march here, for it was so like all our former marches that you would only find it wearisome and *same*. Everything was much as it ever is, except that the heat has now increased to a pitch which it seems impossible can be surpassed,

and although we did not travel by day, the exhaustion I often experienced was even greater
than before.   Two or three curious events happened on the road, which I will however relate ;
one of these was connected with the Baza
people, whom I told you of in a former letter.

The first camping-ground after Haikota was
called Gădâm Bāwa, and on leaving this we
had to pass the Bhitāma mountains, immense
hills of red granite, which the Baza inhabit ; it
was a different part of their country from that
we had passed as we went to Haikota, and on
this occasion we were travelling by night.

There was only starlight, and our men were
terribly afraid.   They constantly made all sorts
of excuses for a rifle to be fired off ; now they
saw a hyena, now they heard a strange noise,
now there was a lion ahead ; their imaginations
were fertile.   Suddenly, just at the very nar-
rowest and most rocky part of the road, I believe
entirely the result of fright, one of the men
lay down and declared he was so ill he could
not go another step.   Neither could *we* halt ;
that would have been too critical.   Almost
without stopping, the wretched individual was
hoisted on to the top of a camel, and as it was
totally impossible to get him medicine at the

moment, the lunch-basket was opened and a
desert spoonful of cayenne pepper was hastily
mixed up with about a tumblerful of water!—
this he was compelled to drink on the spot, and
the cure was so effectual that no other man ever
became ill afterwards at an inconvenient moment.
One of the raids that the Baza are in the habit
of making took place while we were at Haikota.
A herdsman came running breathlessly into
the camp one day to say that two hundred
camels had just been looted by these people.
Immediately all the horsemen in the village
armed themselves and galloped off in the direction indicated, and as there were several soldiers
present, besides the one I have spoken of, the
party to the rescue was not insignificant.   They
very soon found the marauders with the camels
in a narrow gorge, where they had rested, thinking themselves safe from pursuit, but they had
already killed three of the unfortunate animals,
which they were then eating without any sort
of cooking, and before they were even cold!
Immediately the horsemen appeared in sight,
however, every Baza fled, and all the camels
except the unhappy three were rescued.

It also happened that, the morning after we
passed Gădâm Bāwa, a caravan coming up

from the south was attacked under the very hills we had passed by, and four of the camels laden with grain were carried off; but though they lost these, the poor herdsmen made such a good fight that they killed one of the enemy with their spears, losing no life on their own side, and this triumph seemed almost to have reconciled them to the loss of their camels and merchandise.

Our route lay for the most part through a series of plains, surrounded by ranges of very irregular granite hills. The blocks of granite were piled up in confused heaps and masses, assuming all sorts of shapes, and they were of all sizes, and the ground was covered with broken quartz pebbles in every direction. In one of these vast plains, which contained a good deal of low brushwood as well as many tall leaf-less trees, the dogs belonging to the nephew of the sheik started a little hog deer. It was a tiny creature, only about the size of a hare, but it ran with amazing swiftness, giving wild leaps and bounds every now and then, and once it stopped for an instant to cast a momentary glance behind. That moment, alas! was fatal to it. I could not bear to see the chase, and would have prevented it if I could, but immediately the chief's nephew saw the deer start he was off in pursuit, urging on the dogs, and they were all beyond the power of recall in a second. The young fellow was well mounted, and very proud of his horsemanship—never losing an opportunity of either showing it off or of boasting of it—so this was a chance not to be missed. They very soon captured the poor little animal, and I shall never forget the heart-rending little shriek it gave at the instant it was pounced upon. I turned quickly away, and could not but feel that *that* morning's pleasure was greatly marred.

In between the ranges of hills were now and then very steep narrow gorges, and in going through one of these Charlie and his camel very nearly came to grief together! It was a horrid place, and might have been a horrid accident, and makes me shudder even now when I think of it. The hill on one side was almost perpendicular, the path at the foot of it was extremely narrow, and immediately on the other side of the path there was a deep declivity, almost perpendicular also, stretching away into a torrent bed below, which, during the rains, would be one mass of foaming water. Now, however, it was dry, but apparently bottomless all the same.

Suddenly the camel became frightened at something, though we could never tell what, and in its agitation put its foot right into the middle of a great half broken-down bush, the ragged stump of which nearly threw it over. It could scarcely recover itself, but no sooner had it done so than it tried to bolt, and in the plunge it made was again all but over the ravine. I was close by on my camel, of course utterly unable to do anything, and every moment I expected to see both rider and camel rolling over and over in front of me down the gorge. Charlie prepared to leap off, but finally, with great difficulty, got the camel on to a smooth part of the path and all was well.

This was shortly before we reached the next halting-ground, called Aradeb. The name is the same as that of one of the stations I wrote from on the route between Suakin and Kassala, on our journey south. We got to it at eleven o'clock on the morning of the 28th, having marched without stopping since one o'clock that same morning, and having been ten hours in the saddle; so you may imagine that at last I was not sorry to stop. We halted till night under a bower of "miswa" shrubs, and even then did not go on, for I was too exhausted to

move.   My angréb was moved out into the
plain near the rest of the camp, for it was too
stifling and breathless under the miswas, and
once more I went to sleep beneath the stars.
Just as I had settled myself snugly down, all
chance of rest was for a time completely put
to flight by my beholding a huge hyena issue
slowly out of some neighbouring bushes, look
round, and trot quietly past at the very foot of
my bedstead.   Several of the servants saw it
too, so a large fire was immediately lighted, a
rifle as usual discharged, and the men took turns
to watch two together all night.   The night
was deliciously fresh, for we were encamped on
a small branch of the Barka ; and near a river-
bed it was always comparatively cool as soon
as the sun went down.

In the morning, alas! no milk was forth-
coming for breakfast.   Several flocks of goats
were brought down to the river to drink, but
the owners would not spare the servants a
drop, and they returned crestfallen to tell us
none was to be had.   Our cook then tried a
stratagem, which met with perfect success.
He is the man of the Tukruri tribe who
showed us the way to the Settit river long ago,
and he has been cook ever since we last left

Kassala, for there Ahmed was dismissed, as I had told him he should be at El Gwaiya. This Tukruri, Abdul Wahid by name, now put on an old uniform that had been given him by one of the soldiers at Haikota, shouldered an unloaded rifle, and sallied off to try to frighten the people into giving up the milk, by making them believe that he was a member of the dreaded army. They were completely subdued! and that half-negro, Tukruri—about the most unsoldierly-looking fellow that ever stepped —returned in a short time triumphant, accompanied by a boy from the tribe, bringing a large skin full of milk, as, to carry out the fiction, he pretended to have too much dignity to bring it himself.

One more magnificent gorge that we passed through on the last night of our journey I *must* tell you of, for it was such a fine wild place I cannot pass it over. The ravine was full of enormous rocks, over which the poor camels found great difficulty in clambering. Each had to be led separately, and even then they could scarcely get across the boulders. During the rains, they told us, it is always full of foaming torrents, tearing and rushing down it, when it must present a magnificent spectacle. We

much regretted there was no moon, for even
by starlight it was beautiful. It abounded,
in spite of the rocks, with kittar and mimosa
bushes, and in the dim light and uncertain
movements of the camel a long straggling
branch full of thorns, which I could not see
until I felt it, scraped itself over my eyelid,
making a great wound, and for a moment I
really thought my sight was gone! The pain
was excessive for a few minutes, but happily it
was only the lid that had suffered.

The sheik's nephew, who was accompanying
us, was one of those good-natured bores who
are such terrible afflictions in life! He was a
youth of the utmost insignificance of character,
yet ever buzzing round us with silly simper-
ing chatter, evidently believing himself to be
indispensable to our happiness, and, in his
own way, trying to do the polite, poor fellow!
We did not like to snub him, and I doubt
whether he would have seen it if we had; and
in many ways he was useful, so he had to be
endured, tiresome as he was. There were
constant flocks of Guinea fowl on the road, and
his protestations of being able to catch one of
these birds while it was running, himself at full
gallop on horseback, by stooping from his

horse and swooping it up with his hand, were endless ; but though he made an immense détour on one occasion to perform this feat, he did not succeed! He certainly rode at a terrific rate, and guided his horse in and out among the innumerable thorny bushes very skilfully, but he did not get his bird. His servant, however, picked up a small basket, that had fallen from one of the camels, in precisely the same manner in which his master boasted that he would pick up the fowl, yet we had heard nothing previously of this man's prowess.

1st June. The Englishman whom we expected to join us arrived yesterday, and brought the third packet of home letters with him that we have now received. We had had no mail since the 12th of April—seven weeks and a day—so you may form some faint idea of the joy it was to get this one. The newspapers had all been opened, and bore unmistakable marks of having been read, the original covers having been torn off, so that we could not even tell who sent them, but they have come to us in the end, and that is the main point. . . .

The houses that are to be built for us here for the rains are to be of the same sort as those that were ordered for Collalāb, but larger and more commodious, and we were up at five yesterday morning marking out a place for them on a high slope about a quarter of a mile from the village. We have met with a capital house-builder, a very clever fellow, who employs his own workmen, and makes it his regular business. He perfectly understood all we wanted, even comprehending plans which we had drawn out on paper yesterday evening, and he has already sent off his men to the jungles to cut wood and grass,—indeed he said there was not a day to be lost, as the grass is now almost entirely dried up. We found the tukul bête so intolerably hot, owing to the want of circulation of air through it, that the very day after our arrival we had the large tent pitched, and moved into it, shifting the baggage which had been temporarily stowed there back into the hut. I superintended this business in Charlie's absence, he having gone to consult a Circassian officer, who is stationed about a mile from here in charge of a detachment of soldiers, on several points connected with our new settlement.

The hardest work I have had for a long time was to urge these natives, during this move, to anything like alacrity. I wanted to get it all done before the sun became too hot, and I earnestly wished over and over again that I could have shouldered each box in turn myself, and walked off with it to the place it was to occupy, for then it would have been done in half the time. The dilatoriness, the ridiculous chatter, the ingenious excuses for dawdling, were all simply maddening, and again and again I thought of the proverb, " In the East you either learn patience or lose it." I cannot flatter myself that I have achieved the former, but I find the latter of very little use. At last, by dint of cajolery, mixed with slight sarcasms, and finally, more effectual than all, the promise of doubled "bakhshish" if the work were accomplished in time (for which incentive the wily impostors had probably been waiting all the time), I got it done, and I felt in the end as though I *had* moved all the boxes myself, for I am sure I was far more exhausted than any of the lazy men.

4*th*. We had another morning of photographing to-day. First we took an old "Hadji"; he happened to be a priest, and (as the word *hadji* implies) had made a pilgrimage to Mecca. He was a venerable-looking "Father," and characteristically dirty, as all hadjis are. These

devotees seem to wish never to part with the
sacred soil accumulated during that pilgrimage,
so one can but imagine that it has an odour of
sanctity to their senses! This one, to atone for
his *griminess*, wore a chain of splendid beads
round his neck, which in themselves were worth
photographing. After him we took two little
darling boys, with a minimum of raiment that
added greatly to the artistic effect. They were
very handsome and excessively graceful, but
it was difficult beyond everything to get them
to sit still, and at first they were quite frightened at the camera, and thought it was going
to kill them. The hadji and their own father
had great ado to reassure them, and we could
not, as you may imagine, get the perfectly
happy expressions on their faces that we wanted,
after all. Then I tried to induce a group of
women and little girls, who had been looking
on from a distance, to be taken; but when I
went to them and explained what I wanted
they all fled precipitately, screaming—and I refrained from following them — into the dim
recesses of their enchanted castles.

7th. Alas! I am alone again, and shall have
to make the most of my own company for five
or six days, for Charlie is off this morning on

the shooting expedition he has been planning ever since we came. He took Connolly with him, who has had rifle practice daily since his arrival, and who will doubtless be useful in supplying the camp with food, as he has already brought in several hares and some

BIRSCH HUT AT DAGA.

Guinea fowl, although he tells us he never had either rifle or gun in his hand before. Directly Charlie had gone I had a visit from the sheik's wife,—the one here ; for, according to Mohammedan permission, I believe there are several of these ladies in the various encampments ; but this one, I am told, is the chief and most favoured of all. She came surrounded by a numerous retinue of relations and attendants, and they all sat down and had coffee with me, and chatted away quite pleasantly for half an hour. The lady herself was a sweet-looking, placid woman, but had not much to say; a very vivacious little sister-in-law made up for her, however, and did all the talking in a most animated style.

I have found a pleasant diversion very often, during my solitary evenings in different places, in going after five o'clock tea to feed our riding camels. Besides those away with the shooting party, we have three in camp—my own especial " Wad Zaid," one we bought from Herr Löhse, which after him has been named " Karl," and another we got from Sheik Hamed. " Karl" has been taught to amble, and does it to perfection, having exchanged his naturally long step for a gentle easy movement that is delightful. The new one from Sheik Hamed is a good camel too, but young, and not to be so thoroughly relied on as our older friends.

The natives taught me how to feed them. One takes a handful of grain and closes one's fingers almost completely over it, leaving only a little space to allow it to run through where the little finger is doubled against the palm. The same effect may be obtained by joining one's hands together, and leaving a small opening at the lower sides. The camel that is to be fed kneels on the ground and lifts up its head, turning its long face to one side, and, with its mouth almost closed, puckers up one side of its upper lip to make a little hollow tube for the grain to be poured into; and when in this way it has got it all into its mouth, it slowly turns its face round again and munches away with the greatest satisfaction. They love being petted in this manner, and are as gentle and patient as possible while being fed, looking mildly round and waiting quietly till one is quite ready with a handful. When they are not fed like this, they just eat their suppers off a piece of matting on which the grain is placed in a heap before them; in either case they kneel down, and are marshalled in a row beside each other. They have, however, to be watched, for it sometimes happens that one with an epicurean appetite will take a fancy to its neighbour's portion, and a stretch over of its long neck will make sad havoc in a moment of the next heap. Quarrels, indeed, and threatened fights, have now and then arisen from this cause, the intrusion being generally resented with much indignation.

Soon after we came to this place a curious circumstance happened which may or may not speak well for corporal punishment; I don't know what conclusion those who are advocates of the system would deduce from it. We brought a lad of about seventeen with us from Kassala as a servant, whose father had been very useful to us there, and who was very anxious that we should take his son into our service. The father assured us that the boy was equal to any amount of work, and begged that we would not spare him. Musa, which means "Moses," is the youth's name, and while we were in Kassala, and Musa was under the paternal eye, nothing could have been more satisfactory than his conduct. He was all attention to our wishes, and as active as possible. This delightful condition of things lasted even till we reached Haikota, and for a short time after we had been there; but alas! in the vicinity of the two thousand Arabs, among whom Musa no doubt found many a congenial companion of his own age, his good qualities began to wane, and by the time we reached Daga they were completely dissipated, and he was next to useless. No amount of scolding or remonstrance was of the slightest use; Musa was never to the fore, never even to be found when he was called; tasks given him were but half accomplished or wholly left undone, and his idleness began to infect all the rest of the servants; in fact he seemed likely to become the very bane of the camp from laziness and bad example. Many a time at Haikota had dismissal been threatened, but we were then so far from his home that he had probably calculated upon the chance of the threat not being carried into effect; here, however, at last, when his incorrigibleness could one day be no longer tolerated, he was called up and told that he was to leave at once, and be off then and there. As we have now arrived at a point from which the boy could make his way back to Kassala without danger, he was fairly frightened, for he began to believe that he would in truth be turned away, and this was the punishment he feared more than any other. He had the utmost dread of being sent back in disgrace to his father, and would sooner have submitted to any alternative. His own suggestion was that he should be beaten instead, this being the remedy that he was evidently well accustomed to. Imploring that this might be done, he ran with the greatest alacrity to the camel-shed and

returned with a thick kurbatch, exclaiming in
Arabic, " Beat me, Khawajah ; beat me," and
he added in a manner which would have been
naïve had it not been thoroughly earnest, " You
must beat me well, and then I will be a good
boy for a long time to come." . . .

I did not tell you how anxious the people at
Haikota were to receive our empty bottles.
They appeared to consider them priceless
treasures, and offered all manner of things in
exchange for them. Many of the women had
never even seen a bottle before, and looked
upon them with the utmost surprise and
admiration. One poor woman, who had become
acquainted with the marvel the day before,
brought me next morning, in a secret, frightened
manner, a large skin full of honey, with a request
that in exchange I would give her a black
bottle or two if I could possibly spare them.
And when I presented her with three she
seemed to consider the bargain so much to her
own advantage that she was scarcely justified
in accepting it, and I really feared I had begun
to spoil the market.

I must tell you of a chase I had one day on
our march to this place, after a flock of goats, in
the vain hope of getting a little milk. We had

not a drop, and I was longing for a cup of tea, when we suddenly came in sight of a fine herd in the far distance.   They were at the other side of a great plain, by the edge of a thick jungle. We were ahead of the baggage camels, and of most of our foot followers, so directly I discerned the goats I knew we must get the milk for ourselves if it was to be obtained at all.   I proposed a pursuit, but Charlie said he feared it was no use, as, now that all the pasture is dried up, milk is so scarce that the people are utterly unwilling to part with it.   As I, however, wanted only a very little, I thought I should be able to induce the shepherd to spare me a wee drop, so we quickened our pace to a trot.   It was the same story as before.   Directly the man caught sight of us he and all his flock were off in a moment, and the faster he went the faster they all ran. Charlie shouted to him to stop, and held up a piece of money, but to no purpose,—on they sped, and when they came close to the jungle the man just seized up the biggest goat under one arm and darted into the thicket, dodging among the bushes in a manner marvellous to behold. All the rest of the flock skuttered in, helter-skelter too, regardless of thorns and branches, and were hidden from sight directly.   The whole

scene was so funny that the laugh I had compensated in some measure for my disappointment.

12*th.* This is the sixth day since Charlie
left, but I received a note from him an hour
ago, sent in by a *runner*, to say he would be
back this evening, so my solitude is nearly
ended and my mental barometer has experienced, in consequence, a sudden and rapid rise.
My days, during his absence, are always passed
in much the same manner, but both at Haikota
and in this place it has been less possible to get
exercise, as there has been no spot like the
lovely pool at El Gwaiya to go to.   I have not
even had the excitement of tiffs with Ahmed ;
though I have scarcely wished *them* back, even
for the sake of variety.

Sher Ullah has progressed wonderfully in
his lessons, and I have written up letters enough
to last for a year ; but the worst of my letter-
writing is, that as I have but the same tale to
tell to each correspondent the monotony to
myself becomes intolerable ; and, though the
incidents may be new to each one, I would, for
my own sake, give worlds for a fresh set of
subjects to speak about !

A few days ago a party of men from a neighbouring village brought me a little lion, a tiny

cub, which is the dearest pet possible, and makes
a sweet little plaything. It is just like a kitten
in its ways, and only about the size of a full-
grown cat. It was stolen from the lair, poor
mite, while its mother was out on a foraging expedition. The men knew of its existence, and
watched the mother go away, and when she
was safe out of sight and hearing they walked
off with her young one. It does not at all
understand lapping out of a saucer yet, so I
feed it by putting my fingers into the milk and
letting it suck them. Yet it has sharp little teeth
of its own, and claws too, and many is the playful
scratch I have received during a frolic ; but it
means no harm, and is as gentle as possible. I
shall take it home and present it to the " Zoo,"
by which time it will probably be full grown.

.   .   .   .   .

15*th June*. You will be amazed, I am sure,
at the news which will conclude this letter ; and
yet perhaps, after all the changes and uncer-
tainties that my late budgets have told you of,
you will not be very much astonished. We are
to be off this evening, not on our way to any
fresh Arab encampment or river-side settlement,
but *home* again—home to dear old England,
the very name of which, in spite of all my love of

adventure, ever fills my heart with happiness.
Many reasons have tended to this decision,
the two principal being that Charlie does not
find his present rifles satisfactory enough, and
wishes to get others; and, though I have never
told you so before, I have had so many touches
of my old fever again, off and on, especially
lately, that we both think it best I should
escape the coming season; so everything is
once again packed and ready for a start. This
time we are taking a far smaller quantity of
baggage even than when we went to the Gāsh,
and a caravan only just large enough for safety
and convenience. Connolly, who has arrived
most opportunely, is to be left in charge here
of the extra camels, dogs, donkeys, and all the
rest of the possessions, awaiting our return in
the autumn; while Sher Ullah will go with us
to Suakin, and come back with the Arabs when
they bring back their own baggage, and our
riding camels. We shall travel up the sandy
bed of the river Bārka as the smoothest and
easiest route, for we wish to go as quickly as
possible in order to catch the Egyptian steamer
which will leave Suakin for Suez at the beginning of next month.

Our marches will, therefore, be somewhat

forced, and, as I fear I shall be unable in consequence to write to you on the route, my next letter will be dated from Suakin, after we have reached it again.   Indeed, I have just remembered that were I to write I could not send a letter, as we shall be out of the line of the Egyptian mails.   They always go to Suakin by the route which we followed in coming south, quite a different one from that by which we shall now return.   But this last letter from the Eastern Soudan will be sent to Kassala as usual, and forwarded from there as our letters have hitherto been.

LETTER XXXI.

SUAKIN, 3d *July.*

AFTER a fortnight's hard travelling we are back
again at Suakin; indeed, we reached it on the
morning of the 1st, but were immediately told,
to our dismay, that the steamer had gone earlier
than usual—that it had left, in fact, three days
before its time—and that we should have a fortnight to wait before there would be any kind of
vessel to take us up to Suez!

We actually did get off from Daga on the
evening of the 15th of last month, and I bade
adieu, with much regret, to good Sheik Hamed,
for he was a kind friend to the last, and often
expressed a hope that I should return to Africa

in the autumn, when he feels sure that we should meet with better sport. We came all the way through the dry bed of the Bārka, as we had planned to do, marching always by night—though two or three times we were obliged to go on in the morning to get to the wells—till an hour when the heat seemed positively to consume one. On one of these occasions we had been travelling until ten o'clock, and when at last we halted, a circumstance occurred which was an indisputable proof of the fierce effect of the sun. It was about the 20th of June (I cannot remember the exact date, for it was impossible to keep even the smallest diary during this homeward march), and as we had been travelling for many hours after the sun was up, everything on the camels had got baked through and through. We had not brought the Indian tent, but only a light one, which was easy to pitch and did not require many men to put it up, our caravan being purposely as small as possible on account of the quick marching. On the particular morning I am speaking of there was no tree to place the tent under, and in spite of the large ox-hides placed over the top the sun struck in fiercely and was very trying. When my bedding was unrolled and laid down it was so hot from the combined effect of the heat that struck through it from the sand, and the baking it had got on the camel, that I positively could not bear my foot upon a soft cotton wrapper, which was my substitute for a sheet, and really could not avoid a sudden exclamation from the pain! I could not have believed that anything could be so hot and not actually burning, and it seemed almost incredible to me, although it happened to myself. I hustled it away as quickly as possible, and took instead a *woollen* wrapper to lie on, which, strange to say, was far less hot than the cotton one, and not at all painful. The same day, at a later hour, the thermometer stood at 123° in that same tent, so you will perhaps not find it impossible to believe my story.

A circumstance not connected with the heat, but with perils by lions, occurred one evening during this march which made a landmark in the history of our poor Malay boy that, I fear, he will remember unpleasantly for many a long day. We were passing through a thick jungle of tamarisk trees, the feathery branches of which rose high on either side of the very narrow path, and were obliged to go in single file, and when we were well into the midst of this jungle the

men told us that it was thickly infested with
lions. I happened to be at this time on my
donkey, but feeling, as I did before when going
through the gorge near Miteb, that I was in an
unpleasantly low position, I changed and got
on to "Wad Zaid," and then felt happier. I
was indeed glad that I had done this, for a few
minutes afterwards we heard a jackal close by,
barking loudly, and the Arabs assured us that
it was calling to a lion and telling it of the
prey that was close at hand. Charlie fired off
a rifle, and for a moment all was quiet, but
almost immediately the barking began again,
and we knew that both jackal and lion were
still in pursuit. Both barrels were then freshly
discharged, and bullets from them sent whizzing
into the jungle, in the hope that a victim might
perhaps be found unawares. Whether this
happened or not it was impossible to tell, but
all was effectually silenced, and on we went
again. We got through the tamarisk jungle in
safety, and then came a little bit of open ground.
About that period I felt so exhausted that I
said I must stop and have something to *pick me
up!* This was quickly accomplished without
dismounting, and the baggage camels did not
wait; but Sher Ullah, who was riding " Prince,"

and the Tukruri cook, who was on the black
donkey, stopped with us, and then we went on
again after the others. The open space was,
to our surprise, soon closed in by a denser
jungle than before, with a still narrower path
through it; but, as we had heard no more of
the jackal, the thought even of lions had almost
passed from our minds. This jungle was only
a short bit, and Charlie and I, who were going
faster than the donkey-riders, emerged from it
before they did, and got again into an open
space beyond. Suddenly we heard from behind
a terrific shriek, and recognised Sher Ullah's
voice calling out, in Malay, for help. At the
same instant our camels lifted their heads high
in the air and began blowing vigorously; they
had evidently *scented a lion*, and they tried to
run away. We pulled them hard round with
the nose reins and got them steady, and when
Charlie saw that "Wad Zaid" was pacified, and
would behave quietly, he galloped back to
ascertain what was the matter. He found Sher
Ullah alone, looking scared and wild. A lion
had sprung out of the bushes just in front
of the donkeys, which had both immediately
bolted, and as Sher Ullah was sitting carelessly,
and unprepared for a start, he had been flung

over " Prince's " head into, so to speak, the very
jaws of the beast, and found himself on the
ground in the very spot it had occupied a
moment before.   The Tukruri had stuck to
his donkey and been carried off by it into
the jungle on the opposite side.   The lion had
retreated, frightened off by the screaming and
general commotion ; but before Sher Ullah was
well on his feet again he had seen it once
more advancing, and had screamed out more
vigorously than before, when it had again
retired.   The donkeys and the cook were soon
found, the jungle being too dense for them
to get far away, and we put Sher Ullah on
a camel as soon as possible, and did everything
to reassure him, but we could not but feel
a little afraid of the consequences the fright
might have on his brain for some time to
come.

Only once on our homeward route did we
spend an uneasy night from fear of robbers.
We were going through a very lonely part of
the country when our men declared they saw
lights in the far distance and heard voices.   It
was impossible to say whether these proceeded
from another caravan as peaceful as our own or
from a band of thieves, but as we ourselves

were a very small party we did not relish the idea of an attack. Finally, our men declared they were *sure* they were robbers, and became very nervous. We went as stealthily forward as possible, but Arab robbers have ears like hares, and we knew it would be of little use to try to elude discovery. I got my camel close alongside of Charlie's, and asked him *sotte voce* what I should do if we were attacked. "Keep one hand on the nose-rein and the other on your pistol," was the whispered reply that came back,—and with a pulsation not diminished in rapidity, I did as I was told. Soon we halted, the men absolutely refusing to go any farther, saying that if we were attacked we should be safer in a stationary position, and on the ground, than moving; so we halted, but happily were *not* attacked. The drivers insisted on having no fire, in case it should draw observation that might not have hitherto been roused, and in a few hours we were on again. . . .

I grieve to tell you that I have lost my dear little lion; it died one night on the road, from an accident. It had been put into a cage made of wicker-work, which was firmly fastened on the top of one of the camel-saddles, and to secure the animal, the man in whose charge it was, had foolishly fastened a rope round its neck instead of round its body. It got out of its cage in the night, and had evidently slipped on an ox-hide which was below, and not being able to recover its footing on the smooth surface had fallen and been strangled. In the dim starlight it had not been seen; and, if it had uttered any cry, it had not been heard in the general noise of the caravan; but the probability is that, as the rope was firmly fastened to the foundation of the cage, it had been suffocated at once, and when the accident was discovered it was clear that it had been dead some hours. I grieved sorely for my little pet; and, alas! I shall not be able to present it to the Zoological Gardens.

And now I must tell you of the march which brought us into Tokar, and the narrow escape we had of laying our bones on the scorching plain that lies to the south of it, and adding to the list of those who, the Arabs tell us, are yearly buried in suffocating all-destroying sandstorms.

It was the morning of the 29th of June. We had left the river-bed and got out into the plain, but the night had been particularly stifling, and I began to fear that the fever I had suffered from on the Settit was returning again. Even now, that the morning had come, there was an unusually thick parching sensation in the atmosphere, but I was occupied in preparations for the start, and did not observe the horizon. Nearer at hand there was not anything to be seen. We had, however, scarcely finished breakfast when one of the servants came up and muttered something rapidly in a low voice. This caused me no apprehension, for I merely attributed it to some directions that were needed about the packing, and as no particular reply appeared to be given I thought no more of the matter. I afterwards discovered that the man had whispered *a warning*, and that Charlie's wish to prevent my being alarmed had kept him silent. He soon rose, and saying that we had a long ride before us, and that, as we were on the highway to Tokar, through an open country, there was no necessity on the score of danger to keep with the camels, asked me if I was ready to start so that we might get over the journey before the heat became too great.

I rode my beautiful "Wad Zaid" that morning, whose long swinging pace covered the ground with gigantic strides, and I always enjoyed an early march on him thoroughly ; but *his* paces and *my* strength were put that day to a test by which they had not been tried since I had had him.

We started at a walk, but before long the camel that Charlie was riding broke into a trot, and I put " Wad Zaid " into the same pace. We went on like this for some time, when the Arab, who was running before us to show the way, quickened his pace, and we quickened to keep up with him. I have since marvelled at myself a hundred times for my strange, and let me hope unusual, want of apprehension that morning. Charlie (who I fondly believed could never take me in by a hair's-breadth!) said something about "a race with the Arab," and for a time I was actually gulled! How well that I was—how horribly frightened I own to having been when I discovered the truth.

To be overtaken by a sandstorm was the one thing that had always had an insurmountable terror for me ; lions and robbers paled before it. I felt that it might mean an agonising death, and to fall victims to that now, on our way home, after having braved so many other perils, would have been a woeful finale. On the horizon, coming up behind us, was a dense wall of impenetrable dust and sand. It had been scarcely visible in the morning, and even at the time I am now speaking of it was only rising into view ; but the keen Arabs, children of the desert, had descried the long dark line as it lay almost immovable in the early morning, and scented the possible danger. Should the wind rise it would be brought up rapidly, and might sweep over us before we could reach Tokar.

I was as yet, however, unconscious of aught that could be amiss. We were soon going like the wind, and the enjoyment I experienced was an indisputable testimony to the gentle paces of my hajeen. I felt no jolting, and it was not till afterwards that I was conscious of fatigue, and the after fatigue did not nearly equal that which I had often experienced from a long slow march at the rate of two and a half miles an hour. The most remarkable thing about that ride, however, was the way in which the native ran. I could scarcely have believed it unless I had myself seen it. He was an unusually tall man, well and cleanly built, muscular, and without an ounce of superfluous flesh ; had he been picked for the task he could not have been better chosen. We on our camels, and the Arab on foot, fled before

that duststorm at the rate of between seven
and eight miles an hour, for over three hours,
doing nearly four-and-twenty miles in that time,
and that splendid Arab, a model for any sculptor,
and a hero for any racecourse, kept before us
the whole way, and we halted but once on the
road. We had not gone half-way when I
insisted on stopping, fearing that the man
would be utterly exhausted; and it was during
that rest that I discovered the real state of the
case.

We dismounted and sat down among the
undulating ridges of sand on the vast plain, for
the sake of changing our positions for a minute,
and also to have, I must own it, a "pull" at
something sustaining, and in an unlucky moment I turned my head and clearly perceived
what we were flying from. The whole truth
broke upon me, and for a moment I felt
almost paralysed. What if it should really
overtake us! The wind was rising, coming up
as the day advanced, and we were yet a long
way from Tokar. I knew from past experience,
though I had never been exposed to one, how
rapidly sandstorms came up with the wind,
and I confess to having quaked. There was
but one thing to be done. Up again, and press

on as before. The native, who had thrown
himself flat on the sand, was fortified with a
strong draught too, and we were off. I think
we scarcely spoke again before we reached
Tokar ; the one absorbing thought was to get
forward. I was dreadfully concerned about
the servants and baggage camels who were
behind, toiling on at their sluggish pace over
the uneven ground ; but I felt that for their
sakes too the best thing we could do would
be to go on, and, if need be, send out to assist
them, should they be overtaken by the storm,
as soon as it was over.

Shortly before we arrived at the town, however, the Arab slackened his pace and turned
round. He made us turn too, and pointed out
that the wind had unexpectedly changed, and
swept the storm, which had at first set out in
our direction, another way ; the great thick wall
which might have imprisoned us, and shut out
our light and life for ever on the Tokar plain,
had turned southwards, and was now travelling
over the desert away from us, I earnestly hoped
to expend itself in space before meeting with
any unfortunate victims.

The servants, on arriving in the evening,
told us they had come in for the outskirts of it,

and, though that even had been enough to envelop them, and everything on the camels, in masses of dust, there had been no danger. They told us that before the wind had changed they had hurried along the camels at nearly double their usual speed, fearing that the worst would come. Inexpressibly thankful was I as we entered the town ; I could not but feel that it had perhaps been a "race for life ;" it was now over and we were safe, but it was several hours, or I think I may more truly say days, before the effect on my overstrung nerves passed entirely away.

On our arrival we dismounted and were conducted into a rest-house, while the governor was being informed that we were there. This diwan was a mere barn of huge proportions ; but I was thankful to find in it a sort of rustic (*very* rustic) couch, on which, with an ox-hide and my farrwah thrown over it, I was glad to lie down. We had not been there long when the governor came to visit us. He was extremely affable, and said that a house was being prepared for our reception, and ordered honey-water and coffee to be brought while we were waiting. He was followed by a little retinue of attendants, and accompanied by the handsome officer whom we had met before at Wandik, when we were travelling down the country. In about half an hour some of his servants came to say our house was ready, and he led the way to it. We were taken to a perfect mansion!—a mansion, that is, for an Arab town. It was all mud-built, of course, and, from a European point of view, anything but a mansion; but it actually had two stories, rough stone steps at the entrance, and a most imposing gateway, which led into a spacious courtyard. We were taken upstairs, and on the second landing were shown three or four partly stuccoed rooms, each about fifteen feet square, which had been cleared and prepared for our use. They were perfectly clean, having been just swept out; indeed the smell of dust which had been raised had not yet quite subsided. Into these rooms we had the few things which were on our riding camels brought up, and, as the baggage camels had not yet arrived, angrébs were lent us until our own came. On these we rested (I lay down at once and did not stir) until suddenly, to our surprise, a most delightful dinner unexpectedly appeared, kindly sent to us by the courtesy of this hospitable sheik. It was brought in on large wooden

trays, and consisted of a joint of mutton beautifully cooked, and innumerable little dishes,
indescribable but most relishable—there were
cakes and vegetables, pickled mixtures and fruit,
and sours and sweets of all descriptions—and
we did full justice to the repast.

Our fatigues of the morning had perhaps
supplied the zest, without which we might have
been critical and too dainty. After we had
finished, the governor sent a message saying
he would like to repeat his visit, and, though
we privately voted this " a bore," we could not
but respond to his wish. He came, again
accompanied by the handsome officer, and after
we had expressed our thanks for his hospitality
they sat down and entered into a long conversation on affairs relating not only to the Soudan
but to those of Egypt, England, and Europe in
general.

The governor was as eager for information
as the French-speaking Arab at Suakin had
been, and he remained with us till the camels
arrived and our baggage was brought up;
then, after friendly salutations, he left us for
the night. How I longed for repose can be
better imagined than described; but if the day
of our approach to Tokar had been trying, the

night which we passed there was as painful a one as I ever experienced. The twinkling lights in the houses all about, which I could distinctly see from my angréb through the half-closed venetians, were going out one by one; the half-wild Arab dogs, which prowl, and sometimes howl, about the streets all night, were subsiding into unusual tranquillity; the servants rolled up in their cloths, were lying about in passages and courtyard wrapped in profoundest slumber, I even believed that Charlie was unconscious of every mortal care, and I was myself just falling into a condition of peaceful oblivion when I became perfectly wide awake with the most awful sensation of stinging and maddening irritation that I had ever experienced. I was utterly perplexed; this was wholly different from anything I had yet come across in Africa, and I marvelled what it could be. I immediately again thought of fever, for that fever had left a dread upon me never to be forgotten, and I imagined that perhaps the ride of the morning was now having its revenge. I tried to believe it would pass off, and that by remaining quiet the irritation would cease. Far otherwise; it momently increased, till I was nearly beside myself. At last I struck a light,

and I then found that Charlie was as wide
awake as myself, and from the same cause.
Myriads of the tiniest imaginable gnats, things
no bigger than a needle's point, were swarming
around and penetrating deep into the skin. I
had known the same sort of thing in the Malay
Straits from the Malay āgāss,—a horror only to
be known by experience, not description,—but
it had never occurred in our experience of
Africa before. We got out spirits of camphor,
eau-de-Cologne, even spirits of peppermint,
and all such antidotes for ills of the kind as we
carried with us, but to no effect ; the room was
thick with these minute monsters, and till daylight appeared they did not flee away. Then,
fevered in truth and worn out, I got up, feeling
that a bath and the early morning air would
be the best restoratives. The former was soon
prepared in an adjoining empty room, and
never was the luxury of cold water so inexpressibly grateful to my exhausted frame as
then. A cup of strong coffee completed the
restoration, and we went out to see a parade
which was got up specially for our benefit.

A stroll through the town, accompanied by
the governor and several Egyptian officers,
occupied us till the heat became too great, and

we then returned to a substantial breakfast, and after that darkened the rooms and got a few hours of the repose we had craved for during the night.

We found Tokar to be a straggling mud-built town in the midst of a plain, which, now that the hot weather has commenced, is absolutely bare; there is not a blade of grass to be seen on it for miles round; the ground is baked perfectly hard and dry, and dust and sand are blown about everywhere with the faintest breath of wind.

This desolate plain extends far away south, east, and west of Tokar, but to the north the sea is within about twenty miles, and on that side the feathery tamarisk and the thorny mimosa grow still, in some places quite thickly, but in others sparsely, and there are many places that are perfectly bare.

About 5 P.M. we took our leave, bidding a hearty adieu to our kind host, and to all, both officers and attendants, who had contributed to our pleasure and comfort, and set forth again on our camels in the direction of Suakin, "homeward bound." "Wad Zaid" was as magnificent as ever, grand and calm, and quite ready to save my life and his own on any fresh occasion, should he be called upon to do so, and I mounted him once more with redoubled gratitude and pleasure. We made a slight divergence from the direct route to go to the wells, and we loitered there a little. Some of the camels drank, and the water-skins were freshly filled. A number of the natives happened to come up at the moment bringing other camels to be watered, and I remained an interested observer of the busy scene. One more little eventful incident connected with Tokar occurred to me, and it was this. I was so occupied in watching these natives, and in talking to them, that I did not observe that our own party had moved off, and when I happened to look round they were all gone! Tall tamarisks were growing everywhere, and many paths led in various directions, and I could not tell which to take. For a moment I was quite "nonplussed," and did not *quite* like it. Straining my eyes to catch a glimpse of anybody I knew, I suddenly descried Charlie's tall head appearing just above the tops of the bushes, returning to look for me. He had only just discovered my absence; having believed that I had been among the first to go forward, and I am sure he was far more disconcerted than I was when he found I was behind.

A few brisk paces brought us up with the rest, and with only occasional halts for coffee we travelled on during the whole of the night, for it was too fine to lose. The moon was splendid, as she had been on the night of our departure from Suakin nearly five months before, and we could see every step of our way almost as clearly as by daylight. We went on and on for fourteen hours, and when I finally got off the camel I was so utterly exhausted that I lay under a bush in a sort of dead stupor while they were pitching the tent. It was the longest march I had ever had, and following the previous fatigue so quickly had been very trying, but we were marching against time, and it could not be avoided.

LETTER XXXII.

SUAKIN, 14th July.

I MUST send you one last line before we leave this
stifling port, to tell you how very much plea-
santer our stay here has been this time than it
was last February, and how we have been
indebted for this to the hospitality of a most
charming Greek gentleman, a Mr. Maximos,
who has established himself in Suakin since we
were here.   We were sitting in the shop of an
Italian tradesman, waiting to ascertain if our
old rooms in the Pasha's miserable palace were
available, and bemoaning the prospect of two
whole weeks in this Arab town—without even
a journey to prepare for, and no occupation of
any kind to kill the time—when Mr. Maximos,
who had heard of our sudden arrival, appeared
upon the scene, and most kindly insisted on our

coming to his house, and on our remaining with him until the next steamer arrives. As he is living alone, and has not been here long, he has only furnished a few rooms in his house, but these are delicious, and all the appointments of his establishment are thoroughly comfortable. It is so delightful to have floors covered with cool Indian matting to move about on, once more, to have a dinner-table covered with a snowy cloth, and glass and silver shining like mirrors. The cook is an Italian, and his dishes are supreme; all the other servants are Arab women, which is a novelty to me, and the housekeeper, one Miriam, is a treasure. Even here, on the sea-coast, the heat is terrific; and, though not so intensely burning as the inland heat, it is far more unpleasant, being, on account of the nearness of the sea, horribly damp. The atmosphere is filled with steaming moisture, and everything is indescribably sticky and nasty to touch. The thermometer stands at 104° by ten o'clock in the morning, in a large room in the centre of the house, which is shaded nicely by partly-closed venetians and large outside blinds. Later in the day, in this same room, it has been 112° and higher; and one night, on the roof of the house, it stood at 113° at midnight. The natives even are feeling the heat this year more than usual, and several deaths have occurred among them from sunstroke.

Water is now very scarce, and the supply will diminish more and more until the rains commence. Every drop both for drinking and baths has to be bought, and Mr. Maximos told us that, just at present, it is by far the most expensive item in his establishment.

Our evenings have been almost always passed in boating in Suakin harbour, and this has been thoroughly enjoyable. When our host has emerged from his office, and dismissed his clerks, we all go down to the jetty together and have a delightful hour or two on the water. There is often a stiff breeze, and the cool air is most refreshing. The sea near the shore is marvellously clear, and monster jelly-fish are to be distinctly seen below the surface; their hues of purple and green are exquisite, and of every variety of shade. There is a curious long strip of land at the other side of the harbour, which is used as a burying-ground for Europeans. We rowed across to it one evening, and wandered for a bit among the monuments and tomb-stones. They were mostly the graves of those who had died on the voyage home from distant countries; and this island cemetery, in the midst of the sea, on the border of a most desolate country, struck a feeling of mournful desolation to my heart.

On the low flat shore were innumerable hermit crabs wandering about to take possession of deserted shells, and Charlie got his fingers terribly bitten in trying to induce some of these wanderers to occupy certain shells which he thought would suit them. His choice, however, was on no occasion theirs, and I told him to *draw a moral* from the circumstance, but I don't believe he did!

And now I must finish my Suakin narrative with a story which I am sure our charming friend and host will pardon me for relating. He told me this morning that he was nearly drowned in his bath last night! The heat was so intolerable that sleep was impossible, and he spent the whole night wandering about from his room to his bath, and from that to the roof of the house, and back again. He got four times during the night into this bath—an enormous affair, ever so deep, that stands in one corner of his vast chamber ever ready for use—and the last time, utterly exhausted, he went to sleep in it, and woke by finding the water gurgling into his mouth; but he was then almost too dead asleep to recover himself or comprehend the situation. It sounded so dreadful, I did not

like to think of it; but there he was, I was
thankful to see, having escaped the peril and
looking even better than usual!

We shall actually be off to-morrow in one of
the British India line that is now in the harbour,
and we are lucky to catch her, for they say this
is to be the last vessel the company will send
to Suakin.   The harbour is too dangerous for
them to risk their ships in; and I suppose also
that, considering the danger, the freight is not
sufficient to pay them.   Mr. Maximos, I am
glad to say, is going with us (as he is leaving
Suakin for the next few months), so we shall
have the pleasure of his society during our
voyage up the Red Sea.   Our homeward route
will be from Suez to Alexandria, from there to
Sicily, and before reaching England again we
purpose making a hasty run through the continent.   Naples, Pisa, Genoa, Luzern, Zurich,
Geneva, and finally Paris, form a delicious
vista in my mind's eye of a tour which will be
almost as new to me, if not so strange, as that
in the Soudan has been.   We have had time,
while waiting here, to map out this new trip;
and the contrast that it will present to the fore-
going one will but furnish it with fresh zest.

Now that my wanderings in the Soudan are
for the present over, they appear to me almost

like a dream. Constantly while passing through the strange wild scenes of late, I could scarcely believe that they were forming part of my life, part of my actual experience; and, now that we are on the border of civilised lands again, this is more difficult to realise than ever.

The time has been short, but it has nevertheless contained a world of interest, which has more than compensated for the roughing it. I would not have foregone my trip on any consideration; the novel incidents will furnish pleasant memories for many a long day, and the various *contretemps* return even now with amusing force, and often make me laugh. I am really sorry to say "Good-bye" to Africa, and am quite ready to penetrate yet farther still at some future day "across the dark continent;" but whether that prospect will be carried out remains at present in the region of the unknown.

THE END.

www.ingramcontent.com/pod-product-compliance
Lightning Source LLC
Chambersburg PA
CBHW030636030726
47497CB00006B/1810